# PILGRIMAGE

©2013

Written By
## Kurt Winans

Story Concept By
## Brian Schaber & Kurt Winans

Coaster's Quill Publishing

**Coaster's Quill Publishing**
P.O. Box 50583
Sparks, NV. 89435
(775) 200-6966
E-mail: coastersquill@yahoo.com
Website: http://www.coastersquill.com
Facebook: Coaster's Quill Publishing

**Cover Design by**
Portsmouth House Publishing
P.O. Box 583142
Elk Grove, CA. 95758
(916) 599-4942
PortsmouthHouse@aol.com


Printed in the United States of America
First Edition
April 2013

ISBN: 978-1-4507-7499-4

# Acknowledgements

It is the humble opinion of this author, that life could not truly have been lived without the benefit of friends and loved ones that lend a helping hand from time to time. That belief was proven to be correct during the process of writing this book, and I would like to acknowledge a few people in particular for their efforts.

There were dozens of meetings with Brian so that we could discuss and shape our collective thoughts for the content, and then arrive at a desired completion of the storyline. Karl, Renée, and Ken gave of themselves by reading through rough drafts of the text, while offering valuable insight, observations, and suggestions along the way. My wife Cathy was once again a stabilizing force, as she provided an incredible amount of faith and patience throughout the entire process.

The pages that follow, like any other book, represent an investment of significant time and effort. They would not be complete without the assistance of the kindhearted souls that have been mentioned.

Thank you all, Kurt

# 1

## The childhood challenge

It was another typical day during the spring of 1961 in the small dusty central Texas town of Rumley, as Ross Martin lifted his six year-old sister Jessica into the cab of their Grandpa Hank's truck for the ride to school. Ross, who would turn eleven during the upcoming summer, was used to helping his sister whenever he could. In many ways he had been forced to grow up quicker than most boys his age, as some of the daily things that their mother Janet would do for Jessica became his responsibility after she had been taken by the car accident four years prior. This was not to say that Ross had to do everything, but his father Robert was still living in some level of denial about the loss of his wife and Grandpa Hank wasn't as young as he used to be.

Robert was stationed at the nearby Fort Hood Army Base, serving out what remained of his intended thirty year career in the Army. Several years earlier he had enjoyed a promising career much like his father Henry, or Hank as most people called him, but in recent years there had been a fall from grace. There was no way around the fact that Robert needed to keep serving his time, as that was the only source of income and medical benefits for his family. It had been decided, in spite of their sometimes tumultuous relationship, that his father Hank would come live with Robert and the children. After the sudden loss of his wife Janet he needed help with the everyday events of raising two small children, and that help needed to come from someone with available time that Robert also trusted with their well-being. It became a perfect fit in a most unfortunate situation, as Hank was retired and had lost his wife a few years earlier to cancer.

Hank was a proud veteran of World War I, or "the war to end all wars", as a few years after completing college he volunteered for service in 1917 at the age of twenty-four. Choosing to stay in the military after the conclusion of the conflict, he eventually rose to the rank of Army Major Henry Martin before retiring after twenty-five years of service in the early days of the next war. He was trustworthy and dependable to a fault, the kids loved him, and during the almost four years since his arrival, the community had all come to know him as a friendly man in his late sixties that would do whatever he could for a neighbor.

The Wright family, who lived about a half mile down the dirt road towards town, was well aware of Hank's good intentions. Every day without fail, he would stop to pick up their daughter Patty for a ride to school with his own grandchildren. Ross would climb down from the old pickup truck to hold the door open for Patty, and help her into the cab where Jessica would be seated next to Hank. Her mother, Elizabeth, would either wave politely from the front porch, or on occasion present a plate of "thank you" cookies to Hank at the driver side door while the kids climbed into the cab.

Elizabeth Wright was a sweet and somewhat attractive lady whose husband had died during military service a few years back, and often asked how Hank's son Robert was doing. She had offered her help with anything he might need several times over the past year or so, but was unclear as to whether Robert simply didn't pick up on her subtle signals, or didn't care.

Patty was about a year younger than Ross and one class behind him in the fourth grade. Her skin was sun browned by the nearly ever present Texas sun, with long straight blond hair, green eyes, a few freckles, and a smile that would light up a room. She was admittedly a miniature version of her mother Elizabeth, and what mattered the most to her was that Ross thought she was all right as far as girls go. Her look and stature were in sharp contrast to Jessica, who was seated next to her as they headed off towards school.

Jessica was quite a bit smaller as she was only in the first grade, but she had long curly dark brown hair with brown eyes and dimples just like her absent mother. She also had a great smile, which was really special considering the potential lifelong obstacle associated with the metal brace on her right leg.

When Jessica was two years old, her mother Janet had noticed that she was favoring her leg dramatically as she toddled around. A visit to the doctor at the Fort Hood hospital revealed a problem with the development of the bone and muscle structure that would require a brace to help prevent further damage. Jessica was then fitted with a brace that would need to be swapped out occasionally for larger ones as she grew taller until they would no longer be necessary, and began to move around with less effort.

Soon after that was the automobile accident and it took quite some time and effort by her brother Ross to convince her to keep wearing the brace. Her father Robert was in a state of shock over the loss of his wife and Grandpa Hank had not yet arrived, so it was up to Ross to take the lead role for his little sister's well-being. Now almost four years later, Jessica was very comfortable with the brace in all aspects, and had learned from Ross how to put it on and take it off in the same way she had learned to tie her own shoelaces.

As Hank pulled up to the normal spot in front of school to drop the kids off, a few greetings came his way from some of the other folks nearby. He returned the courtesy with a wave, gave Jessica a kiss on the top of her head, and wished the three of them a good day at school. After helping the two girls down from the truck, Ross concluded the daily ritual of leaning back into the cab with outstretched arm to shake his grandfather's hand. Ross had been taught early in his life that proper gentlemen parted company in this way as a show of respect, and there was no other person that he respected more than Grandpa Hank.

With the three youngsters in his care safely delivered to school, Hank set off for Main Street and another of his favorite rituals. Stepping into the diner, he was greeted by the waitress Mable as he headed for the corner table. She followed close behind him with his usual cup of hot coffee, and placed it in front of him as he said hello to his friends. The three other gentlemen already seated at the table were also former military officers who had served proudly, and he enjoyed discussing current events with them on a regular basis.

The main topic on this spring day was the concern over the Russians putting a man into space. Hank had heard the news on the truck radio while on the way to school, but had missed some of the details as the kids were engaged in conversation about homework and such. As one of his friends spoke his mind about how the "red menace" needed to be stopped, Hank suggested that our recently founded National

Aeronautics and Space Administration, or NASA, get busy with trying to catch up with the Russians. He said to his younger group of friends, "The Russians probably won't wait for us in the space race, so we better get busy or face the consequences!" After all, they had already beaten the United States into space with the Sputnik satellite, and had now further added to the insult by putting Yuri Gagarin into a spaceflight that completed a single orbit of the Earth.

After a refill of his cup from the smiling Mable, Hank finished his coffee, said goodbye to his friends, and headed back to the house to take care of other business. Along the way the thought of the future, and mankind exploring space, weighed heavily on his mind, but what he really wondered was what Ross would think about the subject. That evening there was a spirited discussion at the dinner table about the news of the Russian space flight between the two adult generations of Martin men, while Ross and Jessica listened intently with eyes and ears wide open.

# 2

## *The project*

The next few weeks went by without much deviation from the norm, as Lieutenant Colonel Robert Martin would head off to the base every morning shortly before his father Hank would take the kids to school. Hank would meet his friends for coffee at the diner, and then several hours later pick up Jessica from school. Ross and Patty would walk home together after a few more hours of classroom time, and then he would continue down the dirt road until reaching the Martin homestead.

Jessica was always waiting for her big brother on the front porch so they could tend to their chores together, and then they would enjoy whatever free-time was left over. That usually meant that Ross would push her on the tire swing for twenty minutes, while they talked about school and whatever came to mind. At least once a week though, Ross would use his free-time to do some fishing with Grandpa Hank at the small Lampasas River that ran along the end of their property.

On the morning of May 6$^{th}$, a new story about the space race became all the talk about town. As Mable filled the coffee cup with her obvious flirtation, Hank sat with his friends to discuss the triumphant spaceflight of Alan Shepard the previous day. That flight was only suborbital and didn't have the altitude or duration of the Russians previous flight, but it was a huge step in the right direction if America wanted to catch up in the space race. Hank had promised Ross during their customary handshake when dropping the kids off at school that he would gladly discuss the matter with him in greater detail when they were fishing later in the day.

Meanwhile, the teasing in the fifth grade classroom had started up again for Ross. When his teacher began the school day with a discussion about the first American manned spaceflight, Ross had mistakenly verbalized his opinion about how other species could be waiting out there to make contact with our astronauts.

Generally Ross fit in well with his classmates, and had many friends. He was fairly tall for his age with the same brown hair and eyes of his father and mother, and due to his athletic skills was usually chosen early in the lottery of players for football or baseball games. In this case however, it was a different story. This one topic, which Ross felt very strongly about, caused him ridicule from his peers and his teacher every time. His belief that humans were not alone in the universe was not accepted by the general public, so he needed to learn the hard way how to keep his opinions about such matters quiet. Grandpa Hank had warned him several times about discussing such matters in public, but he sometimes just forgot about the sage advice and let his mouth take control of the situation.

That afternoon Ross walked Patty to her house before running the remaining distance home. He quickly did his chores and put off his homework until after dinner so he could meet Grandpa Hank at their fishing spot along the back edge of the property. The secluded spot allowed the two of them to privately discuss the spaceflight of the previous day at length, and the new science project that Ross' teacher had assigned to each member of his class. Like most fishermen, they didn't catch something every time out, but luck smiled upon them this day as they both caught a few nice pan fryers during the two hour session. During the short walk back to the house, Grandpa Hank suggested that Ross take some time to think about how he wanted to tackle the science project. His advice to write some ideas down on paper, collect the necessary materials, and then construct it seemed like a good idea, so that's what Ross decided to do. After all, he had about four weeks to build it and prepare his presentation before the early June due date.

Another few weeks rolled by much the same as the previous weeks, and Ross was busily preparing his science project. He knew most of his class would take the easy way out with a simple design and report, but that's not the way Ross did things. He had several conversations with his father and grandpa about his intent, and they both admired his enthusiasm towards the project. With assembly nearly completed, he asked his grandpa to help him in the barn to see if everything was working properly. Hank agreed to do so, but brought a radio with him so they could listen to a replay of President Kennedy's speech while they worked. It was now May 25th, and the message of that speech made both Ross and Grandpa Hank drop what they were doing to listen. The President had just laid down the gauntlet that he expected the American space program under the direction of NASA to "Land an American on the Moon and return him safely before the end of the decade."

Timing for the daunting challenge couldn't have been better, as Ross felt his science project would really impress the teacher. His plan was to make a scale model of the entire solar system, as opposed to choosing just one planet. He figured some of his classmates would simply paint a ball red and give a few boring details about Mars without really caring. The same could be said about Saturn, which the girls would probably choose because of the rings, but that would at least take a little more effort. In either case the students would probably mention the number of moons around each planet in their report, but it was doubtful they would include them in the model. Ross had gone the extra mile that he had become known for when it came to academics, as his model was massive. All nine planets were represented and to scale against each other with as much accuracy as Ross could manage. They were Styrofoam balls that he planned to paint with the appropriate colors as shown in pictures within the school library's Encyclopedia Britannica, and some orbiting moons were connected to them by pieces of wire. Ross knew the scale of the sun was incorrect, but was prepared to inform the class during his report that the sun would be much larger than the classroom if the planets were the size of the model.

Grandpa Hank thought it was amazing how detailed the model was, but he was unprepared for the best aspect of it. Ross had the idea to connect the planets to welding rods that were fastened to some sort of sprocket under the basketball used for the sun. Each rod went straight out the appropriate distance before a ninety degree turn upwards brought them all onto a level plane with the sun. Ross then showed Grandpa Hank the really cool part, as he began to turn the bicycle pedals by hand that were linked to the sprocket. Each planet began to revolve around the sun before their eyes, and at that instant Hank knew his soon to be eleven year-old grandson would somehow be destined for engineering or scientific greatness.

With the demonstration complete, Ross explained that he still needed to paint all the planets their proper color before the model would be ready for his report. Grandpa Hank said "You will get a fantastic grade on this project even if you don't paint it", and then began to inspect the intricacies of the model. Ross said "Can you help me load the model into the truck and carry it into the classroom on the day of my presentation next week?", and Hank immediately began to wonder if they might have to leave the tailgate down for the ride.

On the morning of the day before his presentation, Ross was feeling great. In drawing names out of the hat several weeks ahead of their presentation dates and times, Ross had been lucky enough to get one of the last few spots of the week long procession by drawing Friday morning. That increased his chances of having the best presentation of the class, as nobody would have the time after his report to alter theirs. The school year would also be completed in another week, which meant more free time for fishing with his grandpa and playing baseball with his friends. As Ross and the girls were getting out of the truck at school, his grandpa asked him if he wanted to go fishing again that afternoon. With a huge smile on his face he agreed to meet his grandpa at their regular spot as soon as he got home from school, and then extended his hand for their customary handshake. Little did Ross know what a great afternoon that would become, as his grandpa had a special gift waiting for him along the banks of the Lampasas River.

Ross ran home from Patty's house as best as he could with an apple pie that her mother had made for the Martin family dessert, and asked Jessica where their grandpa was. She told him that he had gone to the river a few minutes before to get the fishing poles ready, and that Ross should hurry up and get over there. When Ross ran up to the site, he couldn't believe his eyes. Leaning against the old stump that they always used for their gear was a brand new fishing pole and reel with a big red ribbon on it. As Ross shouted out with joy over the gift, Grandpa Hank reminded him that he was scaring all the fish away. Hank told his grandson that he was so proud of him for all the help he had been with Jessica, and the hard work he had done on the science project, that he wanted to give him his birthday present a month early. The only catch was that he had to wait to use it until they went on their four-day camping trip in two weeks at Stillhouse Hollow Lake.

The fishing wasn't very productive that afternoon as they just weren't biting, but the two best buddies had a great time talking about the planets, outer space, and of course the events of 1897 when Grandpa Hank was only four years old. Upon their return to the house, Ross smiled at Jessica and showed her what their grandpa had given him. She returned the smile and told him she had seen it because the fishing pole had been hidden in her closet for the last three days. Soon their father Robert would be home from his day at the base, so everyone got cleaned up and began to prepare supper. As they ate the apple pie that Elizabeth Wright had sent over, Ross relayed a message of good will from her to his father. He appreciated the gesture, and asked Ross to be sure to thank her again the following morning for the kind thoughts.

Ross was awake somewhat earlier than normal, as the big day of his presentation was finally at hand. Jessica held the barn door open as he and Grandpa Hank carefully moved the model towards the old pickup truck. Ross placed his end on the open tailgate, and quickly jumped up to help guide the model into place. Everything about it was perfect in his mind, and he beamed with excitement as they closed in on Patty who was standing by the side of the road.  As he had been instructed the previous evening, Ross ran up to the porch after helping Patty into the cab and thanked her mother again for the delicious pie she had given the family.  Elizabeth asked Ross if his father had enjoyed the pie, and then smiled at the news that he had eaten two pieces.  "The best way to a man's heart …" she thought to herself.

When the group arrived at school on that Friday morning, Grandpa Hank helped Ross unload his model of the solar system that was covered with a sheet, and asked Patty to make sure Jessica made it to her classroom.  Normally he would watch his independent granddaughter walk across the schoolyard and into the room, but his focus today needed to be on helping Ross carry his science project.  Along the way, a few students took interest and began to gather around as they moved towards the classroom.  Grandpa Hank had to eventually ask them all to back off a little to avoid the risk of either dropping or unveiling the hefty object.

Once inside, they placed the model on the table at the front of the class, and Hank moved over to shake the teacher's hand.  Ross was due to deliver his presentation when class began in about fifteen minutes, so he stood by the model to make sure no one peeked under the sheet.  The teacher agreed to allow Ross and Hank to put the model back into the truck when he would return to pick up Jessica, and then Hank left for some of Mable's coffee at the diner.

When Ross unveiled the model and began his report, the teacher stood in amazement at his efforts.  His information about the solar system was concise, and the movement of the planets around the sun when Ross turned the old bicycle pedals was impressive.  If only Ross had known enough to stop there, his presentation would have been perfect.  Unfortunately he pointed out, and began to discuss, a figure of an alien species that he had placed on the small Styrofoam ball that represented Mars.  Almost instantly the teasing from the entire class began in earnest, and the teacher was one of the most vocal.  Ross thought to himself that he would never learn, as no one in this group of people would ever believe such a possibility could exist.  The teacher informed Ross privately that he wanted to see him at lunch time, and that he would speak to his grandfather with the principal about this misguided and disturbing imagination when he returned to pick up the model.

The teasing from his classmates went on throughout the morning, and Ross couldn't wait for the lunch bell to ring. He knew he was going to catch some grief from his teacher and the principal, but at least the constant ribbing from one or more of his classmates every few minutes would cease during lunch break.

Not long after everyone returned to the classroom, his Grandpa Hank showed up to help him remove the model.  As they exited the room, one last round of ribbing from his classmates could be heard.  Before Ross could return, he found himself standing outside of the classroom with head hung low next to his teacher and principal.  Fortunately, his Grandpa Hank was at his side and defended Ross' honor as the topic of his presentation was discussed.  The two men from the school admitted that the work was deserving of an excellent grade, but wondered how such a bright and solid student could believe in the fairy tale of life on Mars.

On their walk home from school that afternoon, Patty listened intently to Ross as he described some of the teasing he had endured throughout much of the day. She was his most trusted friend in their general age group, and he knew he could talk to her about any subject without fear of repercussion. They discussed how well the presentation had gone up until the point where he brought up the concept of alien life, but her reply was one that he didn't expect. Patty informed him that even if he really believed in such life, he should just keep it to himself. The words were strangely close to those of his Grandpa Hank's, which of course added instant merit to their meaning.

Before they knew it, they had arrived at Patty's house to the welcoming smile of her mother Elizabeth. When she asked Ross how his presentation had gone, he replied that it went well and he had received an excellent grade for his efforts. Mrs. Wright was glad to hear the news, and then turned for the house thinking Patty was on her heels. At that moment Patty leaned into Ross to tell him how proud she was of him for not mentioning the aliens to her mother, and then gave him a kiss on the cheek. It was the first time a girl other than his mother or kid sister had done such a thing to him, but he didn't seem to mind. He smiled as she backed away and walked towards her house, and after waiting until she was inside he ran down the dirt road towards his house.

When Ross arrived at the house, Jessica and their Grandpa Hank were waiting for him on the front porch. She held the barn door open again while the two of them removed the model from the old pickup truck and carried it into the workshop area. Ross could tell that his grandpa was upset about something, so he pressed to discover what it was. Hank told Ross that he was happy to defend him against his teacher and principal, but it wouldn't have been necessary if he had just kept his opinion about aliens to himself. He said, "You should always give your teacher the respect he or she deserves, but don't trust that particular teacher with any aspect of your bright future. Just finish your last week of school in his class, and then move on to more open minded people." What Hank didn't tell Ross was what the teacher had said to him while Ross was helping Jessica into the truck. Although the principal didn't agree, the teacher felt that Ross should discuss his vivid imagination with a psychiatrist as soon as possible.

That evening the family enjoyed a nice dinner, which was topped off by what remained of Mrs. Wright's excellent apple pie. Grandpa Hank announced that he and Jessica were going to make Ross a special Saturday morning breakfast in honor of his excellent grade on the presentation, and take them both to a movie later in the day if they got all their chores done in time. Ross thought that was a great way to start off the final weekend of the school year, as he smiled at his adorable little sister.

# 3

## *Sounds from the kitchen*

Bounding down the stairs after a lengthy sleep, Ross found Jessica and their grandpa hard at work on a breakfast fit for a king. His place at the table was already set, and Jessica had picked some fresh daisies from the garden for the center vase. Their father Robert was still asleep, and Grandpa Hank informed the two of them that he probably would be for quite some time. After the children had gone to bed the previous evening, Robert had fought another battle of depression with the bottle over the absence of his wife Janet. Although he was always in top shape for duty at Fort Hood, the extra time at home on the weekends occasionally led to such an event. Jessica asked Ross to sit down, as she and grandpa would take care of everything. She brought him a glass of milk, while Grandpa Hank brought over a plate of homemade biscuits and gravy with sausage and eggs on the side.

The three of them had another great time together, and the food kept coming until Ross could hardly move. He thanked them both for the fantastic breakfast, and their efforts on his behalf, then stood to do the dishes. Grandpa Hank said he would take care of the dishes if Ross would do him a small favor in return. The pie plate of Elizabeth Wright needed to be returned, so Grandpa Hank thought it would provide a good opportunity for Ross to help his sister with some exercise for her bad leg. Ross was glad to take on the chore, because he knew Jessica needed to keep exercising if she ever wanted to get out of the brace, and he could visit with Patty by doing so.

With pie plate in hand, the two of them set off on the trek down the dirt road. Ross was careful to move slowly enough that Jessica could keep up with him, but he also wanted her to press the pace a little bit. About twenty minutes later they arrived at the home of the Wright's, and walked through the gate of the white picket fence. Ross knocked on the front door, and Patty soon answered with her customary smile. A few seconds later, Elizabeth arrived while wiping her hands dry on her apron, and invited them to sit on the front porch for a spell. It was rare that Jessica would walk that far without stopping, so Ross graciously accepted the offer so his little sister could rest before the return.

What took place a short time later caught them all by surprise, as sirens could be heard approaching from a distance. Rumley was a quiet town that was rarely disturbed by the shrieking sounds of sirens, so people took notice when they were heard. Soon the sheriff's car and an ambulance created a long trailing dust cloud as they roared by on the dirt road. At that point there was only one place they could be heading in such a hurry, and Ross instinctively knew it was bad news. He turned to Mrs. Wright, and asked if she could keep an eye on Jessica while he found out what was going on. He needed to run home, and he could cover the distance in significantly less time without his sister by his side. Elizabeth gave a positive silent nod, and then shouted her support to the family as Ross was through the front gate in a matter of seconds.

Robert Martin had smelled his father Hank's great cooking from his upstairs bedroom, but had not stirred in time to join the group for breakfast. More than an hour had gone by since the aroma of biscuits and gravy had wafted into his room, and he wondered if there were any leftovers for him to enjoy. As he lay in bed attempting to shake away the cobwebs of the previous night's depression, he heard the loud noise of crashing dishes from the kitchen below. Thinking that Jessica or Ross had dropped something; he got out of bed and made his way to the bathroom for his morning ritual. A few moments later he exited his room and made his way to the stairs, but heard no sounds of the mess being cleaned up. Robert called out the names of his children and father while descending, but once again was greeted with silence.

Feeling somewhat perturbed at the lack of response, he arrived at the bottom step and slowly rounded the corner into the kitchen. His pace then instantly quickened, as his father Hank lay on the floor with broken dishes surrounding him and the tap water still flowing at the kitchen sink. Kneeling next to the motionless body, he attempted to bring him back to consciousness, but Hank was pale and unresponsive to the efforts. Robert quickly sprang to his feet and raced for the phone to get some help. Within five minutes he heard the distant sound of sirens approaching, but it would make no difference as Grandpa Hank was already gone.

The sheriff pulled up to the house in a cloud of dust with the ambulance just seconds behind, while Robert stood waiting for them on the front porch. He waved them all past as he informed the medical team that the body was in the kitchen. As Robert strode in behind them, the sheriff began to ask him questions of how the events had unfolded, and if anyone else was in the house. At that moment Robert realized that he didn't know the whereabouts of his two children, and the only person who could shed some light on that particular question was lying dead on the kitchen floor. With a new cause for panic, Robert began to call out their names while frantically searching the house. The search soon led to the outside area of the property with the help of the sheriff, but it seemed unlikely that the kids would be hiding with all the commotion currently at hand. Just then Ross came running past the tire swing in a full sprint, and he didn't even slow down until his father arrested his movement at the base of the front porch steps.

Ross was greeted with multiple questions concerning where he had been, and did he know where his sister was. Through a series of half sentences as he tried to regain his breath, Ross informed the sheriff and his father of returning the pie plate, and Jessica's security at the Wright's house down the road. Then it was his turn to ask some questions about the ambulance and his Grandpa Hank, but the verbal answer of the horrible truth became unnecessary as the medical team emerged from the house with a sheet covered occupant on the gurney. The men from the ambulance reported to all present that it appeared to be a massive heart attack, and there was nothing that anybody could have done for Hank. The news was shocking to Ross, whose last words to his grandpa had been along the lines of "See you in a little while." Hank had been so full of life just a short time before as they ate breakfast together, and now he was gone forever.

With the body loaded into the ambulance, Robert assured the sheriff that he would come down to the hospital later that day to fill out whatever forms were necessary, but first he would need some time to gather up Jessica and have a talk with his two children. The sheriff nodded with agreement, and then followed the ambulance towards the hospital.

Jessica was the first to notice the return of the two vehicles that had sped towards her house, but this time they drove by slowly with no sirens or lights turned on. Elizabeth Wright tried to get the attention of the sheriff as he drove by, but Robert had asked him not to do anything that might tip off little Jessica. Elizabeth knew all too well the meaning of an ambulance returning from a scene at a slow and quiet speed. Either everything was just fine, or the worst had happened. She also knew that whatever the case may be, she had an extra little girl to watch over until informed differently.

Following the suggestion of Ross, Robert agreed a long walk to clear his head was in order. That would ultimately be safer than driving over to the Wright's place and it would give the two of them a chance to discuss how to break the news of Grandpa Hank's death to Jessica. The time to cover the half mile walk was somewhere between the deliberately slow pace Ross had set with Jessica, and the frantic sprint of his return to the house. During the walk Robert and Ross had one of their best conversations in recent years. It was just a shame that such a devastating circumstance had been necessary to create more of an open dialogue between father and son.

As they opened and moved through the front gate, Elizabeth stood from the bench on the front porch. In an act of pure habit she smoothed the front of her dress to become more presentable for her company, but she knew it was wasted motion. The facial expressions of Robert and Ross showed her that her appearance would go un-noticed because the worst had happened.

Patty and Jessica were playing inside the house, so Ross was sent in to retrieve them while the two adults conferred.

When they all returned, Robert picked up Jessica and put her in his lap as he sat down on the front porch bench. A few seconds later she was crying in her father's arms, and Ross began to weep as well. He had been strong up to that point fearing that crying was a sign of weakness, but he knew that Patty and her mother wouldn't hold it against him. A short time later Robert thanked Elizabeth for keeping an eye on Jessica, and she offered the service anytime he needed help. In spite of her leg now being rested enough for the walk home, Jessica rode home with teary brown eyes on her father's shoulders as the three of them trudged onward in quiet contemplation.

# 4

## *Taps*

News of Grandpa Hank's death spread through the town quickly, and the weekend went by in a blur. Robert had contacted Fort Hood to request some emergency leave for the arrangements of the upcoming funeral, and the elementary school had been notified that Ross and Jessica would be absent at least one day during their final week of class.

It was very strange for Ross and Jessica on Monday morning to be riding to school in their father's car as opposed to Grandpa Hank's truck, and Ross got a blank stare from his father when he reached out his arm for the parting handshake. At the diner, Hank's friends whom he shared coffee and conversation with every Monday through Friday raised their cups in tribute to a fallen veteran, and Mable shed a tear.

The funeral had been set for Wednesday morning before it got too hot, and the majority of the town came to the cemetery for the service. Before leaving the house that morning, Robert had a few quiet moments with Ross. He handed him a necklace with a small shiny emblem attached that had belonged to Grandpa Hank, and informed Ross that it had been his grandpas wish that he be given the necklace when he passed away.

Ross had of course seen the necklace many times before, and had spoken to his grandpa about the origin of the emblem on several occasions. He thought it had been a secret between the two of them, but apparently Robert knew all about the origin as well. Ross immediately put the necklace on, and

22

then loosened his shirt and tie so that he could wear it inside of the clothes just as his grandpa had always done. Robert patted his son on the shoulder as Ross readjusted his tie, and then asked him to go check on his sister.

The family sat together in quiet reverence as the color guard from Fort Hood carried the coffin to the gravesite. One of the many arrangements that Robert had taken care of during recent days was to ensure that his father received a proper military funeral. Retired United States Army Major Henry (Hank) Martin would get the sendoff he so richly deserved, because his length of service during both war and peacetime had earned him such an honor. The only miscalculation on Robert's part was the twenty-one gun salute, as the loud noise had startled Jessica and made her scream.

As the American flag draped upon Hank's coffin was folded with precision into a white star-filled triangle of blue, the solemn sound of taps was played by the lone trumpet player nearby. All the retired and active duty military personnel in attendance snapped to attention and saluted their comrade in arms, while Mable, Elizabeth, and many of the other women shed several more tears.

The flag was then presented to Hank's son Lieutenant Colonel Robert Martin on behalf of a grateful nation, while Ross comforted his little sister. Robert then stood in front of Ross to present the flag to him, and whispered into his ear a message that would resonate for years to come. He told Ross that his wish was for him to keep this flag for the remainder of his life in remembrance of the sacrifices that his grandpa had made for America, and that he someday pass Robert's burial flag onto one of his own children in similar style. Ross stood and saluted to accept the honor of the flag, while pledging aloud to fulfill the desire of his father. It became crystal clear to him at that instant what his destiny would be, and he had his grandfather to thank for the motivational inspiration.

# 5

## A day of transition

On the morning of June 7th, 1968, Ross made sure the necklace that once belonged to his grandpa was safely tucked inside his shirt collar, as he fastened the top button and adjusted his tie. Due largely in part to the upcoming event, this particular Friday was going to be better than most, and he wanted to get on with it. Now standing a few inches over six feet tall, the seventeen year-old was about to complete the last compulsory event of his high school years by delivering a speech during commencement as the valedictorian of his graduating class of fifty-one students.

Jessica soon appeared at his bedroom door to see how her older brother was doing, and gave him a big smile and kiss on his check before fine tuning the knot of his tie. Even though the tie was already perfect, she couldn't resist the temptation because Ross had done so many things over the years to assist her. The team of brother and sister had grown even closer throughout the past seven years, and had learned how to rely on each other more than their father. That in effect made this day of celebration for Ross somewhat bitter sweet for Jessica. Her big brother was about to graduate high school, and in a few weeks' time would leave town for his appointment to the United States Naval Academy in Annapolis, Maryland. Although that represented a tremendous opportunity for him, she was concerned about how she would do without him being around. At least Patty would still be in town for one more year to help Jessica with the transition into high school.

As the two of them made their way downstairs, their father Robert was waiting for them. He smiled and said how proud he was of both of them for how mentally strong they had become. Although there had been times in the past when he had let them both down, today he was completely sober and focused on the upcoming graduation and ensuing celebration.

Robert informed the two of them to let Elizabeth Wright know he would be along to pick her up in a few minutes, as she had agreed to sit with him during the ceremony and then be his date for the party afterwards. Although no romance had ever blossomed between the two of them over the years, they had become closer friends as the relationship between Ross and Patty had become romantic. Elizabeth had also been a tremendous help in raising his daughter Jessica since Grandpa Hank had passed away, and Robert was grateful that she was around to help with some of the challenges that a girl goes through as she becomes a young woman.

For what would be the last time, Ross and Jessica climbed into grandpa's old pickup to go retrieve Patty for the ride to school. In spite of still wearing the brace on her right leg, Jessica no longer needed help getting in and out of the truck as she did when she was a little girl. Even so, Ross still held the door open for her as he had been taught by his grandpa.

As they slowly approached Patty's house to avoid kicking up a lot of dust, she stood from the bench on the front porch where she and Ross had spent so much time talking about the future. Patty was wearing the same light blue dress that she had worn to the prom a few weeks prior, and looked beautiful with her long blond hair pulled up and back for the special occasion. Jessica climbed down from the truck to greet her while Ross delivered the message from his father to Mrs. Wright, and then returned to hold the door open for his girlfriend and little sister. During the previous few years after Ross had learned how to drive, the three of them had gone to school every day in the old pickup as they had done before Hank had passed away. The only difference now was that Jessica had a window seat because Patty wanted to sit next to Ross as he drove.

Once they arrived at school, Ross headed for the gymnasium to gather with his fellow graduates, while the two girls made their way through the crowd to locate four good seats for the commencement. Their path was not a direct one, as a few young men wanted to speak with Jessica along the way. She had just completed the eighth grade and was beginning to turn all the boys' heads. The long curly brown hair, big smile and dimples that had made her such a cute little girl, had now been enhanced by the development of some curves on her body and additional height. All the attention Jessica had been receiving lately made her feel good inside, because it wasn't just about the leg brace like it had been when she was little. Patty informed her that some of the boys in high school would be mature enough to look beyond the leg brace, while others still needed to grow up some, and it would actually be a great way to find out if they really liked her or not.

Robert and Elizabeth soon joined the young ladies in the seats, and a few minutes later the procession of graduates walked down the center aisle. This was one of those mornings when most local businesses in town were closed, because seemingly everyone wanted to be at the ceremony. Amidst all the other pomp, an introduction was made for Ross as the valedictorian of the class of 1968, and he rose to deliver his speech.

Deep down Ross knew that most of his classmates would remain close to this little dusty town of Rumley, or perhaps venture to other parts of Texas, but he couldn't wait to spread his wings. His speech brought forth the possibilities that lay within each of the graduates if they only gave themselves a chance to succeed, and that some of the terrible social events that had recently occurred within the country should not dampen the spirit of this youthful generation.

Just two months before, Dr. Martin Luther King Jr. had been assassinated in Memphis, Tennessee and much of the nation was still currently in shock over the assassination of United States Senator Robert Kennedy. That tragic event had been recent enough that the funeral had not yet taken place. Little did anyone in attendance know that the social unrest to which Ross spoke of would be magnified in the upcoming months with riots in several cities across America including a large one surrounding the Democratic National Convention in Chicago, Illinois.

At the conclusion of his speech, his two favorite girls stood to applaud and most of the gathered crowd followed suit. Ross had become the first student from Rumley to ever receive an appointment to attend one of the military academies, so it was quite fitting that he be given the honor of a standing ovation. He graciously accepted the honor with a hint of blush in his cheeks, but was more gratified with the free apple pie a la mode that he had received from Mable at the diner the previous afternoon.

With the graduation ceremony complete, many of the townspeople gathered for a large picnic on the football field, while others, such as Mable, needed to return to their jobs. Perhaps for the first time Robert realized that his little girl was growing up, as several different boys gathered around Jessica while Ross and Patty stood close by. Elizabeth reminded him that Patty would help look out for her in school, but that Jessica would be just fine because Ross had prepared her with some sage advice about many of the boys. The celebratory picnic was scheduled to go on for several hours in the hot Texas sun, but eventually the Martin and Wright families would slip away for a more private celebration.

# 6

## *A farewell to innocence*

The next few weeks went by in a flash. Ross and Patty had joined most of the graduating class for a three day camping trip to Proctor Lake that began on the day after graduation, which was a journey of slightly less than one hundred miles to the north of Rumley. They had been there privately, or with a small group of friends, for camping several times in the past, and it was a place that Ross and Grandpa Hank had planned on visiting before he passed away.

At the time of his death seven years prior, the dam was under construction to create the man-made lake, and the two of them couldn't wait to try the fishing. Instead the memories of the campground by the lake belonged to Ross and Patty, and it would always hold a special place in their hearts as that was where they had both experienced physical love for the first time. Proctor Lake had also been the location of several deep conversations about plans for the future, including Patty's hopes to attend the University of Maryland when she concluded her last year of high school.

At least fifty people showed up for the after-graduation camping trip, with the majority of that number being represented by couples. It was somewhat like attending the senior prom wearing bathing suits instead of formal attire, but Ross and Patty had a wonderful time during what they knew would be the last days of innocent freedom with this group of people. One night while sitting on the beach stargazing, Ross made the comment to Patty that he wanted to go into space someday.  The Apollo missions of the current day were making tremendous progress, and it would only be a matter of time before NASA fulfilled President Kennedy's dream as put forth in his speech that Ross had listened to with Grandpa Hank in 1961.

Upon their return to Rumley, Ross did all that he could with his few remaining days helping out around the ranch.  He wanted to get Jessica set up correctly for life without him being around, and that meant doing as many heavy chores and repairs as possible.  He saw very little of his father Robert during those days, and spent as much time with Patty as he could.  Knowing how in love with Ross her daughter was, Elizabeth Wright gave them as much space as possible during those final days.

Before he knew it, Ross was standing outside of the general store waiting for the bus to arrive.  Many people had come to wish him a fond farewell, and he had plenty of snacks for the long bus ride from kindhearted souls such as Mable and Elizabeth.  He shook his father's hand while asking him to be patient with Jessica, then turned to her and hugged her tightly while lifting her off the ground as he had done so many times over the years.  She giggled when he tickled her ribs, and then smiled as she wished her big brother a safe journey.  Jessica had promised to keep the fishing pole and their grandfather's American flag safe for as long as Ross needed, and he knew she would protect them.  Because of Grandpa Hank's death just two days after giving Ross the fishing pole, it had never been used.  The red ribbon was still attached, and Ross had secretly vowed to keep it that way for as long as he lived.

The final goodbye was the most difficult of all, and everyone else knew enough to back away and give the two young lovers some private space.  Patty was doing her best to hold back the tears, but she was losing the battle. They held each other in a long embrace while sharing a passionate kiss, and then she presented Ross with a letter that he could open after the bus pulled away.

When the driver informed Ross that it was now or never, he gave Patty one final kiss goodbye and stepped onto the eastbound bus. He found a window seat near the back, and slid the panel open to wave as the bus began to move away. With luck he would see all of these people when he returned for Christmas break, but that was several difficult months into the future. His final glimpse of Patty and Jessica provided Ross with some comfort before the bus turned the corner, as the two of them stood together in a sisterly embrace.

# 7

## A new challenge

Indoctrination day at the United States Naval Academy in Annapolis, Maryland was intense to say the least. The first of what would become perhaps several thousand lessons over the next four years was that Ross Martin was now a small fish in a very large ocean. Everyone associated with the academy, be it administration, faculty, or midshipmen, were incredibly bright, and he was at the bottom end of the food chain. Ross now understood part of why his father had said he was proud of how mentally tough he had become, because he would need to keep his wits about him if he hoped to pursue his dreams.

When room assignments where handed out to the incoming class of midshipmen, Ross found himself placed with three other plebes, or freshmen, that had come from various backgrounds. He was the last to arrive at his typical four person living quarters, so his choice of bunk was pre-determined. As Ross said hello to introduce himself, one of his roommates stepped forward with outstretched hand. James Franklin seemed like a friendly guy from Seattle, Washington who was a couple of inches shorter than Ross, but probably outweighed him by twenty pounds. He was a soft spoken black man who had grown up in an area of the country that had far less racial tension between blacks and whites than the other two of his new roommates.

Next to approach was Shaun Jamison who was from a tough Irish neighborhood on the south side of Boston, Massachusetts. The street smart kid was small and thin in stature, but Ross instinctively knew he could probably hold his own in a fight.  He also figured that Shaun's focus on succeeding would be intense, because the academy may have been his best chance to escape from the negative aspects of his home town.  At least in that regard, they already had something in common.

The last of his new roommates to step forward was Davis Lee Wakefield III from near Charleston, South Carolina.  He came from a wealthy family, and was the only one of the group that surpassed Ross' six foot-two inch frame, but his introduction made Ross well aware that he had more growing up to do.  Davis Lee, as he insisted on being called, said he was glad to have another "southern man" in the room, and claimed that he and Ross had to stick together because the other two roommates were "Yankees!"  His next statement made even less sense, as he informed Shaun that he needed to switch bunks because the two men from the south should be on the same side of the room.

That sentiment did not sit well with the young man from Boston, who had been the first of the four to arrive and had already squared away most of his gear.  Ross immediately quieted the situation by saying, "We are all going to be living together for the next four years, and this is not the best way to start things off."

With the peace temporarily restored, Ross took the empty bunk next to James and began to unload his gear.  He thought to himself that this plebe year would already be difficult enough, but it could become next to impossible if the four of them couldn't get along.  He had been in his quarters roughly five minutes, and had already learned another lesson of diplomacy while also demonstrating leadership abilities.  Those were facts that had not gone un-noticed by their squad leader who had been listening to the introductions while patrolling the hallway.

It didn't take long for Ross to acclimate to academy life. He enjoyed the rigors of the academic pace needed to survive, and seemed to fit in well with many of the other midshipmen. The days and weeks went by quickly, with the help of multiple letters and care packages from Patty and Jessica, and soon he was stepping off the bus in Rumley for a short Christmas break. Jessica tried to give Ross and Patty as much space as possible during their limited time, but the three of them enjoyed some fun times together. She and Patty had really become more like sisters since Ross had left for the academy, and because of that Jessica had transitioned into high school with relative ease.

Elizabeth Wright invited Robert Martin and his two children over to her house on Christmas Eve for a good home-cooked holiday meal that had been prepared by Patty and herself. The five of them had a really good time, but the highlight of the evening was gathering around the television set after dinner to watch the broadcast from Apollo 8. That mission had just become the first manned spacecraft from Earth to orbit the Moon, and Ross was saddened that Grandpa Hank had not lived long enough to see it happen. The event in itself was the next big step in the effort to eventually land a man on the Moon, so Ross was watching with great enthusiasm. The broadcast from the three astronauts further solidified Ross' intent to someday travel into space.

During the last evening before his return bus trip to Annapolis, Patty informed Ross that she had been accepted to the University of Maryland in College Park just outside of

Washington D.C.  It was great news as she would be much closer to Ross again starting the next fall, and as he earned liberty from the academy they could spend time together.

Upon his return to Annapolis, Ross and his roommates quickly readjusted to the disciplined environment of academy life.  There were some difficult moments as would be expected with four young people from various backgrounds, but for the most part the remainder of the school year went by without any problems.  Eventually every plebe has to arrive at the realization that a team effort is needed in order for everyone to survive.  Some struggle with academics, while others face challenges with the physical aspects that are required, but with some help from the team all can pull through.

The only one of the group who seemed to occasionally have difficulties with that concept was Davis Lee, as he had been raised to believe that someone of James Franklin's color, or Shaun Jamison's heritage, was inferior to his own.  He had let it be known to all who would listen that he, along with his father and grandfather, had been named after Confederate President Jefferson Davis and Confederate General Robert E. Lee.  The socialization, or brainwashing, of his outdated southern belief system had been firmly embedded throughout his youth, and it represented the negative side of what otherwise could be a nice bright young man.

Ross took the opportunity during every skirmish between his roommates to impart wisdom and show leadership abilities, but was also careful not to overstep his boundaries.  After all, they were all grown men and it wasn't his responsibility, or right, to dictate their actions.

# 8

## *Her big day*

Soon the plebe year, or what's generally known as the toughest of the four at a military academy, was over and Ross was headed home to Rumley for another short break. His bus arrived in town the evening before Patty would celebrate her graduation from high school, but she was unaware of that fact. In what had been an acceptable lie, Ross had informed her that he would be in town in another week.

The only reason he would even be able to attend the event was because her 1969 graduation was scheduled to take place one week later in June than Ross' had been the previous year. That meant that Ross would obtain summer leave from the academy at the completion of his plebe year in time to fly to Dallas before riding on the bus to Rumley. Patty's mother Elizabeth would keep her occupied so that Robert and Jessica could pick him up at the general store undetected, and then on the following day he would sneak into the seating area with the others while the graduates gathered in the gymnasium. Ross' plan was to surprise Patty when he would be the first one to stand and applaud at the conclusion of her speech as the valedictorian of her class.

Everything about the plan worked to perfection, and while Ross slouched next to Jessica so he wouldn't be seen by Patty, she gave him a gentle elbow to the ribs. She didn't miss the opportunity to pick on her older brother a little bit by reminding him that Patty was the valedictorian of a larger class of fifty-three graduates, and was therefore smarter than he was.  Ross took the ribbing, both literal and verbal, in stride, while informing Jessica that her own class might be larger still. He said, "That should be considered additional motivation for you to strive for the same goal that both Patty and I have achieved."

Ross was the first to stand at the completion of Patty's speech, and applauded her effort.  She beamed with delight at the sight of him, and kept her eyes fixed in his direction for the remainder of the ceremony.  When the two of them finally had a chance to embrace at the conclusion of the commencement ceremonies, little doubt was left that they belonged together.  A few well-wishers came by to see how Ross had been doing at the Naval Academy, but he quickly reminded them that this day belonged to Patty and the rest of the graduating class.

The two of them decided to forgo the camping trip with her classmates to Proctor Lake, because they wanted to use the extra time to get Patty ready for her great adventure.  A few weeks later Ross and Patty boarded the bus together for the trip east.  His summer leave would be over soon, and she was anxious to look around her new school in Maryland that was less than fifty miles away from Annapolis.

# 9

## *Tossing of the cap*

Over the course of the next three years, Ross continued to excel at the Naval Academy. During their second year together he had developed a stronger friendship with James and Shaun, but Davis Lee continued to create occasional problems. Unfortunately every time he returned to South Carolina, or spoke to his father on the phone, the ancestral hatred of others was reinforced. Not even the tragic event that befell upon Shaun during the summer after their second year at the academy could bring him around.

While on summer leave back in Boston, Shaun was simply in the wrong place at the wrong time, and it cost him dearly. A stray bullet from a robbery at a convenience store had left him in a wheel chair for the remainder of his life, so his dreams of becoming an officer in the Navy came to an abrupt end. It was a shame that Shaun had found a way to escape his neighborhood, and was on the path to a more productive life, only to be accidentally shot while picking up a few groceries for his mother just two blocks from the family home. She probably would never forgive herself for sending him to the store, but Ross knew the random act of violence against her son was in no way Mrs. Jamison's fault.

Ross, along with James and Davis Lee, had traveled to Boston and visited Shaun in the hospital after they had been informed of the event by their squad leader, but he wasn't exactly in the mood to listen to any of Davis Lee's immature bigotry about the neighborhood where the shooting had taken place.  Shaun was happy to see both Ross and James, but let it be known that he was much more receptive to the idea of either one of them coming alone for future visits.

As graduation day approached, the three remaining roommates were each looking forward to their respective future postings.  Many events of both a positive and negative nature in society had occurred during their four years at the academy, and there had been numerous discussions among the young men about several of them.

Heading the list of positive achievements for America, and frankly all of mankind, was the successful landing of ten men on the surface of the Moon.  The historic event had first been accomplished by Neil Armstrong and Buzz Aldrin on the Apollo 11 mission during July of 1969, and had been duplicated successfully on four of the five other attempts since that particular flight.  The only miscue had occurred during the Apollo 13 mission when a near fatal explosion in the spacecraft while in flight made a landing on the Moon impossible.  Fortunately for the astronauts, a large team of highly skilled and dedicated personnel at NASA were able to get them safely back to Earth.  There was still one more Apollo mission to the Moon that was scheduled for December of 1972, but all other future missions had been cancelled due to budget constraints.

On the negative side of the human endeavor had been the tragic massacre at Kent State University in Ohio during May of 1970.  While hundreds of college students were in the midst of a protest against the United States military presence in Vietnam, four of them had been killed, with several others wounded, by gunfire from the National Guard troops that had been sent in to subdue the unruly behavior.  It had been an emotional event to say the least, and had stirred deep feelings and opinions from both sides of the argument during the discussions in their quarters.

In the most recent weeks, the discussions of worldly events had been overshadowed by talk of each man's respective assignment, or posting, after graduation. Davis Lee, through the assistance of his powerful and well-connected father, would be stationed in Norfolk, Virginia. That way he would be out of harm's way, and close enough to the family that they could maintain their influence over his thought process. Ross was again saddened by the fact that Davis Lee had actually made significant progress towards accepting other people, but that progress would soon be reversed by his family.

James Franklin had decided to become an officer in the Marine Corps, and while his choice was something that had earned him the respect of others, that path would potentially place him in harm's way. He would most assuredly find himself in the middle of the Vietnam conflict that was still ongoing.

Ross had decided early in his academy days, and frankly long before that, to become a Navy pilot and fly jets. He had completed his major course of study in the field of aeronautical engineering, and had jumped through the appropriate hoops to make that ambition a reality. He, like James, would be headed for the Vietnam theatre, but at least Ross would be based on the relative safety of an aircraft carrier.

The other good friend that Ross had at the academy was Dennis Strickland, who was a year behind him as a member of the class of 1973. He was from a family in Colorado that had been in the mining industry for the last three generations before him, so he justifiably excelled in the field of geology.

Both Dennis and Ross had similar ambitions with regard to career path, as the collective plan was to fly jets and then apply for the astronaut program at NASA. When Ross had once asked him why he just didn't go to the Air Force Academy in his home state, Dennis informed him that it was because the Air Force Academy was in his home state. In short, he wanted to escape the nearby family influence and become an individual.

Patty was completing her third year at the University of Maryland, and had been discussing the possibility of working on a post graduate degree after finishing her current course of study. Neither she nor Ross had returned to Rumley since the day they left on the bus in the summer of 1969, but Patty had done a pretty good job of keeping abreast of the news back home via letters or telephone calls. She routinely gave Ross any updates from home that concerned Jessica or anything else that seemed important, but the town had not surprisingly stayed pretty much the same. The news of one sad event had been delivered to them during the past winter, as the dear sweet old Mable from the diner had died.

It had been a pleasant surprise for Ross when Patty's mother Elizabeth and Jessica had come east together a few times to visit, but Robert had not come with them. They, with Patty's help, had convinced him to come out on their next visit when Ross would graduate from the Naval Academy. It was a huge day in the young man's life, so the three women had badgered Robert relentlessly about the need for him to attend until he reluctantly agreed to do so.

Both Ross and Patty were sorry that they would miss Jessica deliver her speech as valedictorian for the class of 1972, but they were confident that she would do well. As Ross had predicted, her class was larger than either one of theirs with sixty-two graduates, so Jessica was sure to remind them of her superior intellect when she next saw them. Her acceptance to Rice University in Houston, Texas was a well-earned reward for all of her hard work and dedication, but Ross was not yet willing to admit that his little sister was smarter than he was.

One of Jessica's graduation gifts was for her to be fitted with a new leg brace. The technology of such devices had come a long way during the fifteen years since her first brace, and her leg had become much stronger over the years. Ross wasn't really convinced she still needed a brace because her limp had become much less pronounced, but it seemed to give her extra confidence with daily activities.

When Ross tossed his cap into the air with his fellow graduating midshipmen during the 1972 commencement at the United States Naval Academy, he had the same four people in attendance as had been there when he graduated high school. His father Robert and sister Jessica were staying in a hotel near Patty's apartment, while Elizabeth settled in with Patty.

Ross had asked that he and Patty be allowed to have a quiet dinner by themselves the night after graduation, and then the five of them could spend the next day together doing whatever came to mind. He was sure that the ladies would all have something to talk about that next day, as his plan was to present an engagement ring to Patty after the meal. Much like their quiet times back at Proctor Lake, Ross and Patty discussed plans for the future that included career opportunities and a desire to someday start a family of their own. In spite of the obvious direction of the conversation, Patty was still surprised to see Ross kneel down next to the table while fumbling with a small box. He looked in her eyes and said, "Will you do me the honor of becoming my wife?" To which she excitedly said, "Most definitely!"

Luckily for Patty her mother was already asleep when she returned to the apartment, so keeping the secret of their engagement until the following day became much easier. She even went so far as to remove the ring before going to bed so her mother wouldn't see it in the morning, and then put it back on while she wasn't looking when everyone gathered for their day of sightseeing and fun. As predicted, the excitement level could be heard from quite a distance when Jessica was the first to notice the diamond on Patty's finger.

After a few weeks of post-graduation leave, which was spent entirely with Patty, Ross headed off for flight school down in Pensacola, Florida. He would go through rigorous training for twelve months, and then receive another short leave before being deployed to Vietnam. It was during that break in the summer of 1973 that he and Patty were married, as she had just recently graduated from the University of Maryland. Ross had asked his good friend Dennis from the academy to be his best man, while Patty's good friend, and fellow student at the university, Betty Collina would stand as her maid of honor.

Ross knew Betty well from the multiple times that she and Patty had come over to watch him play baseball for the Naval Academy varsity team. Back in Rumley he had played both football and baseball during his high school days, but his talent in football wasn't sufficient enough for him to play at the university level of competition. Betty's first look at Ross had been from behind as he warmed up for the game. Patty had pointed out his number 51 on the back of his jersey, while also informing her it was the same number he wore in high school, but it was several minutes before he would turn around and notice the two young ladies in the bleachers. Dennis, who had also just graduated was on leave before beginning his own stint at the flight school down in Pensacola. He was also acquainted with Betty, because the four of them had double dated a few times in the past. There was no romance to speak of, but it made the events surrounding the wedding more comfortable because of the familiarity.

Ross and Patty had their wedding ceremony in a church east of Washington D.C. with very few people in attendance, but Elizabeth and Jessica were there. They had once again showed their unwavering support by making another trip east from Texas for the happy event. Once again Robert, who had just retired from his thirty-one years of active service in the military the previous winter, was absent. That came as no real surprise to Ross, or Patty for that matter, as it had been a major endeavor to have him come east just once during the previous five years.

They had precious little time for their honeymoon before Ross was compelled to report back to duty, but they made the best of it. Although it wasn't the most joyful of topics, their final deep discussion before his departure was centered on what would happen if Ross was killed in action. As his wife, Patty would be entitled to certain benefits from the military that would include a death benefit payment. The money would be of little comfort if that event came to pass, but at least Ross knew Patty would be somewhat taken care of.

# 10

## Deployment

Ross boarded the transport plane at Andrews Air Force Base near Washington D.C. with many other young men from various branches of the military, and took his seat for the flight to San Diego, California. From there he had a much longer flight to a base in the Philippines near Vietnam, which included a short stopover in Hawaii. During that brief time on the ground Ross never had a chance to leave the airfield, as the intent of the military was to simply refuel the aircraft, change out the flight crew, and allow the men a brief walk to stretch their legs.

When Ross reported to his duty station aboard the USS Enterprise, he could hardly believe it had only been a few days since the time of waking up in Patty's arms. He would of course miss her terribly, but he also knew he had to keep his mind on the task at hand or he may not be lucky enough to see her again by surviving the upcoming year. Ross also thought his posting on the Enterprise to be appropriate because he wanted to someday venture into space. He had occasionally watched a television program throughout the previous few years that had portrayed mankind on deep space exploration aboard a fictitious ship with the same name.

As a young Ensign with not much flying experience, Ross knew he could learn quite a bit from almost all of the other pilots aboard the ship. He paid close attention to anything the instructional pilots, or I-P's, would be willing to teach him so he could become a better pilot, and had soon earned the respect of a few of the senior pilots for his efforts.

One aspect of Ross' pre-flight ritual was to always grasp the emblem on the necklace that had belonged to Grandpa Hank. He would rub it with his fingers for good luck before removing it and zipping it into the lower pant leg pocket of his flight suit. Ross had to remove the necklace because regulations dictated that pilots not have any jewelry around their necks while flying, as it could interfere with the throat microphones needed for communication purposes. Ross would also take a moment before each mission to speak silently with Patty back home in the states. He knew these types of rituals were common place for pilots, so he never worried about being teased for doing so. The process helped him relax before being launched from the flight deck, which was important if he were to do his job correctly.

By the time he had completed his one-year tour of duty onboard the aircraft carrier, Ross had been credited with shooting down four enemy planes. He had also taken part in numerous missions to bomb bridges or railway lines used by the enemy, and had been bumped up one step in rank to Lieutenant JG, or Junior Grade as it is known, for his stellar work.

In late June of 1974, Ross headed home to his wife Patty whom he hadn't seen since their ever so brief honeymoon after their wedding a year before. During that time she had decided to leave the Washington D.C. area, and had returned to her southern roots in Texas. Patty had taken a job in the Houston area so she could be somewhat close to Jessica, and was really enjoying that city as opposed to her days in Washington D.C.

Although she had made some good friends while in college, especially Betty, the main reason for attending the University of Maryland was to be near Ross. Since he was no longer at the Naval Academy, she decided to return to an area of the country that felt a little more like home to her. After all, there had never been a time in her life except after Ross had graduated from the academy that she wasn't living near at least one of the Martin children.

In the meantime, Jessica had just completed her sophomore year at the nearby Rice University, and had loved every minute of it. Her leg still gave her a little trouble from time to time due to all the extra walking associated with campus life, but it was getting stronger and the brace helped. There had been little time for young men in her life with her busy schedule, but she did enjoy looking at the much more diverse selection that Houston offered as opposed to Rumley. Occasionally she went out on a date, but ultimately her studies were more important to her.

When Ross stepped off the plane, Patty almost fell to the ground. She was so happy to see him, and looked skyward to say thanks for delivering him safely back to her. He had gone through the entire year on the USS Enterprise with nothing more than a cut from shaving, but he knew there were many more servicemen less fortunate. A few pilots in his squadron had been lost when their planes had been blown out of the sky, and a few more that had needed to parachute out had probably been captured by the enemy. A fate that some considered worse than death, but how could anybody really know?

At the same time that Ross strode confidently towards his wife, other soldiers and sailors were coming off the plane to their loved ones with devastating injuries that would change their lives forever. Ross knew instantly that he needed to get Patty away from that scene as quickly as possible, because there was a good chance he would be called back into action for another tour of duty.  Prolonged exposure to those types of visuals would only do her harm, and he didn't want her to be concerned with any of the terrible "what if" scenarios.

Their joyous reunion was brief, although thirty days together was a wonderful change when compared to the short duration of their honeymoon.  As Ross had predicted, he had been selected for a second deployment to Vietnam, so they would have to make the most of his short leave.  The many letters both had written to each other over the previous year had been of great comfort, but it wasn't the same as waking up next to each other every morning.  They got together with Jessica on a few occasions for dinner, but for the most part they just enjoyed each other's company as they rekindled their romance.

# 11

## The second tour

By the end of July, Ross was back aboard the USS Enterprise for his second tour of duty. He hadn't been gone long enough to forget the daily routine, so getting acclimated to life at sea again wasn't difficult. Throughout the next year Ross had seen a few more pilots die, or potentially get captured by the enemy when shot down, but he had been fortunate in his lone mishap.

After recording his fifth overall kill by shooting down an enemy plane, his plane was badly damaged during the same dog fight. There had been roughly a dozen planes from each side involved at the beginning of the aerial combat, but the squadron from the Enterprise had knocked five of the enemy planes from the sky before it was over. The victory had not been without cost however, as one plane from the Enterprise had been blown to bits along with the damage to Ross' plane.

There was enough left of Ross' plane to fly away from territory occupied by the enemy, but it was doubtful he could make it back to the aircraft carrier. Ross knew if he could manage to at least get well out to sea before the plane broke apart, his chances of avoiding capture would increase. He took great care, as he nursed the wounded aircraft to keep it aloft for as long as possible. The squadron leader, Commander Harris, had stayed by his side off the port wing after sending the remaining planes back to the Enterprise, and he knew that the damage to Ross' plane was too severe to attempt a carrier landing. Even if Ross could somehow cover the entire distance, he would still need to ditch in the ocean somewhere near the ship. Unfortunately for Ross, he didn't make it that far as the plane began to shake violently during what would become the last few minutes of its life. The controls then became totally unresponsive, and he radioed to Commander Harris that he would need to eject.

With his transmission understood and verified, Ross watched as his escort plane peeled away to a safe distance before he pulled the ejection handles located over his head. He was launched into the air high above the smoking plane with tremendous force, and then his parachute opened an instant after he began to fall back to Earth. During his slow descent towards relative safety, Ross watched his plane crash violently into the sea below. With no pilot to fight the controls, the plane had nosed over into an almost vertical plunge downward. It was easy to follow the path of the plane, as a trail of black smoke coming from the damaged craft stood out boldly against the surrounding light blue sky. Ross wondered if he had been trailing that much smoke since he was hit, or had it become that pronounced only during the last few minutes before he needed to bail out. He spotted Commander Harris circling around him as he drifted towards the water, and a gentle rocking, or wave of the wings, signified that his position had been relayed to rescue personnel. Ross realized how lucky he had been to make it this far out to sea, and then braced for an impact with the water that would create a mighty splash.

For the first time in his life Ross finally understood how vast the oceans of the Earth were. He had always gazed upon them from the comfort of the beach, a ship, or various planes, but he had never been this isolated and at the total mercy of the waves before.  Ross had followed the protocol of cutting loose the parachute after hitting the water, and swimming away from it so as not to get tangled up in the guide lines as it filled with water and sank.  Once at a safe distance, he then untied and kicked off his boots.  The idea behind that was to ease the strain on the floatation device, and his legs, by getting rid of the excess weight, because a pilot never knew how long he would be in the water.

Three hours after watching Commander Harris fly away towards the Enterprise, Ross began to wonder when the rescue helicopter might arrive.  During that time of helplessly bobbing in the waves, Ross had several quiet conversations with Grandpa Hank, Patty, Jessica, and even his father Robert.  He was actually thankful for his present situation, because it was most definitely better than if he had needed to eject over enemy territory, or had been killed when his plane was hit.

The peace and tranquility of his quiet contemplation over his relative luck was then interrupted by the sounds of helicopter rotors in the distance, and Ross knew he would soon be hoisted from the water.  A moment later he shot off his flare to help guide the helicopter to his exact location and soon after a rescue swimmer jumped into the water roughly fifty feet away from him.  A basket was then lowered, Ross climbed in for the ride upward, the rescue swimmer followed suit, and off they went.  It was a long slow ride back to the Enterprise, but Ross didn't mind as he knew he was lucky to be alive.

Once back on the deck of the ship, Ross was greeted by Commander Harris and a medical team.  He would spend the next few days in the infirmary recovering from his near miss, and all the guys from his squadron came by to visit him from time to time.  By collecting his fifth overall kill of enemy aircraft Ross had officially become an ace, and had therefore earned himself a recommendation by Commander Harris and the Captain for another promotion to full Lieutenant.

Before he could climb into a new jet fighter and fly again, Ross needed to be cleared to do so by the medical team and Commander Harris.  He had suffered no serious injuries such as broken bones or burns when his plane had been shot down, and none of the high-powered rounds fired by the enemy plane had struck him either.  The odds were that if one had, Ross would not have survived long enough to get his plane to relative safety.

Ross demonstrated both the physical and psychological ability that was needed to fly again to the satisfaction of those who would make the decision, and he was cleared to fly.  Some sage advice then came his way via Commander Harris, as they discussed his brush with death.  He suggested that Ross not inform his wife or family members about being shot down until after he returned home.  It wasn't the type of thing that should be put in a letter, and it would only make his loved ones worry about his safety more than they already did.  Ross knew he would worry more about Patty if she had added cause to worry about him, and that would diminish his skills and sharpness while flying.  He still had roughly eight months remaining on his second one-year tour, so he needed to stay focused.  With that in mind, Ross heeded the advice, and kept the news from Patty until he got home.

The remainder of his tour was successful without any more trouble in the sky, and the wonderful news of the end of hostilities came his way four months before the completion of his tour. Ross had managed to get one more kill by shooting down another enemy plane roughly a month after he had suffered the same fate, which brought his total to six enemy planes shot down during the two tours.

Perhaps of more importance to Ross than the number of kills, was the feeling of redemption. Ross knew that the pilot he recently shot down was probably not the same one that had put him onto the ocean, but he needed to think it was in order to obtain some measure of closure.

# 12

## *Safe in her arms*

By early August of 1975 Ross was on his way back home to Patty. The long transport flights that had taken him across the vast Pacific Ocean towards his duty station near Vietnam paled in comparison to the ones that brought him back home. He knew the flights were no different; they just seemed much longer because he was anxious to see his wife again.

Patty joined a large gathering of people who were waiting for their loved ones near the tarmac, and jumped for joy when she saw Ross emerge from the plane. As had been the case a little over a year before, he was unharmed compared to some of the less fortunate who had come home on the same flight with him.

Ross helped a young wounded soldier down the stairs from the plane, and then walked with him over to his family. After wishing him well he turned to begin the search for Patty, but there was no need as she was standing only twenty feet away from him. Ross said, "Hello beautiful" as he began to move towards her, and then she lunged into his arms. From Patty's perspective, all was right with the world once again, as Ross had been safely delivered back to her in one piece.

Throughout the previous year, much of the social unrest that had become a trademark of life in America during recent times had calmed down considerably. Without a doubt, the most significant event to take place in the country during that time had been the resignation of Richard M. Nixon in August of 1974. He had the misfortune of getting caught up in a scandal that went all the way to the oval office of the White House, and then he became the first President of the United States to surrender his office before either death or expiration of term. Because the former Vice President, Spiro Agnew, had resigned amid the same scandal sometime earlier, the current Vice President had not actually been on any ballot. That led to another first in American history upon Nixon's resignation, as Gerald Ford became the first President of the United States to have not been elected to either one of the top two spots in the executive branch of the government.

The other significant change in America was how the military was treated upon their return from foreign conflict. Ross had heard first hand from his father and grandfather that they, along with their fellow soldiers, had been welcomed home with open arms after World Wars I & II, and similar respect had been given to those who returned from the Korean conflict. The Vietnam War however, which had been the catalyst for much of the recent social unrest, had been a different story.

For the next thirty days Ross would be on leave, so he and Patty once again made the most of it. She had no idea where his next posting would be, but Ross had assured her he wouldn't be going back into a combat scenario like Vietnam. The two of them discussed many things during the next few weeks, including Ross having been shot down. Patty was initially angry with him for keeping the information from her, but then understood his reasoning once he explained the situation to her.

As the time grew closer to the end of his leave, Ross received a letter with his new orders. Patty was at work when the letter arrived, so he took a deep breath before opening it.

Ross was very excited with the contents of the letter, and rubbed the emblem on his necklace as he thought about how he could surprise Patty with the news when she got home.

That evening over dinner, Ross informed Patty that they would have to give up the apartment and move for his new posting. His leave had been extended an additional week, but he would have to report for duty on Monday, September 15th. They could live together in the housing on base because it was a non-combat location, and if they didn't have everything packed up by the time he needed to report she could join him at a later date. Patty was in no mood to be separated from Ross again, and vowed to be ready in time. She then took a deep breath and asked him where they would be moving to.

Ross beamed with excitement, as he revealed that they would only need to move about fifteen miles from their present location. He had been accepted into the astronaut program at NASA, and the bulk of his education and training would take place in Houston, Texas. It was the most wonderful news for both of them, as Ross could pursue his dream of going into space someday, while Patty could keep her present job and the friends she had met since relocating to Houston.

The housing subdivision that they moved into near the Lyndon B. Johnson Space Center was occupied by several other astronauts and their families, so they felt an instant connection with many of their new neighbors. As they began to unload their possessions from the moving van, Patty asked Ross which room he intended to use for his new office. He walked through each room of the house, and then placed his fishing pole with the red bow still attached and Grandpa Hank's flag in the corner to signify he had reached a decision.

On his first day at NASA Ross realized he was definitely one of the youngest pilots in the astronaut program, but he had apparently received a few letters of recommendation to help pave the way. He would soon begin what would become many years of rigorous training for something that only a very elite group of people in America were chosen to do. The work would be challenging, but the reward would be something that Ross had wanted to do since his youthful days of talking about space with Grandpa Hank.

# 13

## The long wait pays off

Ross sat at one end of the long table that had all six members of the mission crew facing the media. It had been six and a half years since the day he became an astronaut in September of 1975, and he would finally be going on a flight into space as a mission specialist aboard the space shuttle. Ross would be thirty-two years old in a few months, and had worked hard to get where he was. Another promotion during that time had made him a Lieutenant Commander in the Navy, and he was still young enough that he might be able to make multiple flights into space.

The past several years had been filled with great news for Ross and his family. He and Patty now had a four year-old daughter named Aurora who had arrived on November 16, 1977, and Patty was due to deliver a second child in a few months. Jessica had finished her degree at Rice University in the spring of 1976, and had continued on to law school. She was now working at a firm in Houston, so Ross and Patty had a chance to get together with her often.

They were both very proud of Jessica, but Ross thought there were two drawbacks to his younger sister's prowess. For one, he would probably never win another argument with her as she fine-tuned her trial techniques whenever she could, and two was that she now had a new reason to keep the leg brace on. Ross tried to explain to Jessica that she would get more respect as a good lawyer without pulling on the jury's heart strings, but law school had taught her to take full advantage of any opportunity that may present itself. Ross thought her leg was fine and she had become a beautiful young woman of twenty-seven who was destined for success, yet she continued to rely on the leg brace.

Most of the questions from the media in attendance were directed at the mission commander or the pilot, but Ross and the three other members of the crew were there for the sake of team unity and photographs. This would be the last of such gatherings for the benefit of the media, as the crew of the shuttle was scheduled for launch in less than a week. When this briefing was over, the crew would soon be on their way to Cape Canaveral for final preparations.

Ross was actually surprised when one of the reporters directed a question at him about the payload of the mission, but he showed his poise by answering completely without rambling on. As the crew rose to exit the room, a few senior members of NASA were in the adjacent corridor discussing Ross. He was unaware of it at the time, but they were adding his name to a list of candidates for a future mission.

It was all Ross could do to keep from screaming "Yee-Haw" as the space shuttle Challenger pulled away from the launch platform during the early morning hours in March of 1982. The awesome power and amazing technology associated with launching something of that size and weight into space was unequaled, and he was enjoying every second of the bumpy and jolting ride. Ross' steady vital signs had not gone un-noticed by the flight surgeon and senior members of NASA. The monitors revealed that all the vital signs of the other five astronauts were racing wildly from excitement, fear, or outright panic, while Ross remained calm throughout it all.

Eventually the ride began to smooth out, and soon the Challenger reached orbit as planned. The mission of five days was a complete success, and the spacewalk that Ross and one other crew member needed to perform in order to assist in the deployment of a communications satellite went perfectly.

Ross couldn't help himself after the task had been completed, as he lingered outside of the shuttle on a tether looking down at the Earth for as long as the mission specs would allow before reluctantly coming back inside. As they were helped out of their spacesuits, Ross had a huge smile on his face that couldn't be misinterpreted. He had finally made it out to space, and he wanted to come back again as soon as the crew rotations would allow for it.

Once again the crews' vital signs rose or sped up considerably as the shuttle became a ball of fire during re-entry into the Earth's atmosphere, but Ross was smiling from ear to ear. There were easier ways to leave Florida on the east coast and arrive in the desert of Southern California five days later, but this had been a much more spectacular way to do it. The Challenger shook violently as it fought its way back towards Earth, and Ross just rolled with the punches.

Safely back on terra firma and at "wheels stop" on the long runway of Edwards Air Force Base in the Mojave Desert, Ross couldn't help it as he said, "Let's do that again!" The statement broke the tension that all had felt with the landing, and would be one of the last things recorded on the official transcript of the flight. Ross had gained some notoriety with the mission commander and pilot for his work before and during the mission, but was still unaware of how much he had impressed some of the senior staff by his actions.

The debriefing of the crew went well for all involved, and NASA was pleased that the communications satellite was sending back a strong signal. Before long the astronauts had all been returned to Houston, and Ross was welcomed by the warm embrace of his wife and little girl.

Less than three months later Patty gave birth to their second daughter, as Rachel joined the family on June 11, 1982. On the day that Rachel turned three months old, more good news came along. Ross had been selected to join the crew of another space shuttle mission that was slated to launch in slightly less than a year. His preparations for that flight would be significantly different than his previous mission, as he had been selected as the shuttle pilot for an August 1983 launch.

# 14

## Window seat

The next eleven months went by quickly. Ross had been very busy with his training for the upcoming space shuttle mission; while Patty had her hands full back at the house just trying to keep up with the needs of their two little girls. Rachel had celebrated her first birthday a few months back, and Aurora would celebrate her sixth before Thanksgiving rolled around. Jessica was also becoming more and more involved with the law firm, so the opportunities for the three adults to get together were difficult to come by.

On this occasion, Ross occupied a center seat at the long table that faced the media corps less than a week prior to launch, but he handled the spotlight well. He, and the mission commander, were the target of the majority of their questions, but Ross would divert a question to another member of the crew if it was more applicable to their task while in flight. Ross believed it was important for the media to understand that all members of a crew are equally important to the success of a mission, and they deserved as much of the spotlight as he and the mission commander. It was just one more aspect of his leadership abilities that had caught the attention of the senior staff at NASA.

Four days before the launch a new experience awaited Ross at Cape Canaveral, as the mission commander had asked him to come along on a short walk. The two men were not alone during the walk, as a few NASA technicians were also close at hand, but Ross knew very few others had been invited to take such a stroll. They walked along side, or sometimes behind, the giant crawler platform that moved the shuttle at a painfully slow pace out to the launch site. The wide road that leads from the VAB, or Vehicle Assembly Building, towards the two different shuttle launch pads is a few miles in length, and the journey takes the crawler several hours to complete. After a few hundred yards of the up close view, Ross and his commander had seen enough. They headed back inside the VAB as there were many other tasks to be tended to, and time was growing short.

Ross rubbed the emblem on his necklace one more time for good luck before being helped into his spacesuit, and had a quiet moment of thought with Grandpa Hank. A short time later a few technicians strapped the crew down tightly into their seats and Ross was grateful for the assistance. With the shuttle in a vertical position for launch, he thought the most difficult aspect of a mission was climbing into a seat that would have him on his back while wearing a spacesuit that was extremely cumbersome in full Earth gravity.

With a thumbs-up from each member of the crew, the hatch was sealed, the countdown was called out, and the shuttle began to vibrate as the attached rocket engines came to life. Slowly at first, and then with ever increasing velocity, the shuttle Atlantis tore away from Earth's gravity. All systems were working according to specifications as they climbed higher and higher into the sky, and then the sky around them turned black as they entered space.

Three of the members of this six person crew were first-timers into space, while Ross was the only one who was on his second voyage. One mission specialist in the back seat was on his third ride, and Ross would help him with the spacewalk he was due to take in a few days. The mission commander was on his fourth, and by his own admission last, ride into space. He was ready to become an instructor for the younger generation of astronauts that was coming up, but had earned the right to command a mission before doing so.

The five days of the mission were extremely successful, and Ross flew the shuttle through the fireball of re-entry to a perfect landing at Edwards Air Force Base in California. This time at "wheels stop" he closed the official transmission of the flight with a sentiment of, "Man this thing is fun to fly", which got a laugh from those seated around him.

Throughout the debriefing process of the flight, each member of the crew had praise for Ross and how helpful he was with their respective challenges while in space. They all had experiments to complete, or spacewalks to perform, but all the training in the world was no substitute for someone who had actually been there to do it. The mission commander had also privately informed the senior NASA staff that he believed Ross was a natural to someday command a future mission. Ross was unaware that the endorsement had just moved him to the top of what had already become a very short list.

After some well-deserved vacation time with Patty and their two little girls, Ross returned to work at NASA. The shuttle program was beginning to move along nicely, and several items on NASA's orbital missions' checklist were being accomplished. In early November of 1983, a few weeks before his daughter Aurora's sixth birthday, Ross was called into an office to discuss a future mission. NASA intended to retrofit one of the space shuttles in the fleet of five for a different type of mission, and they wanted Ross to be the commander of the flight. He was overjoyed at not only the chance to go back into space, but also the chance to command the mission. Ross accepted the offer from the senior staff without waiting for any of the details, and then rose to shake their hands. The group of men smiled as they knew the correct choice had been made, but asked him to sit back down so they could inform him of the mission at hand.

Ross leaned forward in his chair as they told him of the planned retrofit to the space shuttle, and the secrecy of the mission that would be two years away in November of 1985. They continued by saying that the crew would consist of Ross and one other man yet to be determined, with a hopeful duration in space of twenty-one days.

With an eyebrow raised from the information he had just been given, Ross stated that "No other space shuttle mission to this point has exceeded a week in space." He knew that the current design specifications of the space shuttles allowed a maximum of two weeks in orbit because of restraints on fuel and materials such as food and water. Ross had no doubt that longer human durations in space were possible, as both the Americans and Russians had proven in the past with their respective orbiting space stations, but not on a shuttle mission. The senior staff then informed Ross of the most exciting news he could ever receive, as the true intent of the mission was further laid out for him. Very little time would actually be spent in Earth orbit, as NASA had decided it was time to return to the Moon.

# 15

## A temporary secret

Throughout the next eighteen months Ross kept the news of his pending mission from Patty and everyone else. All those on the outside of NASA who knew him thought he was helping train other astronauts for flights, while waiting his turn to hopefully be chosen for another mission himself.

During that time Ross had been promoted again to full Commander in the Navy, and his crew mate had finally been selected. It was his old friend Dennis Strickland from their days at Annapolis who had been accepted into the astronaut program about two years after Ross, and Ross had been the one who suggested him for the flight. As had been their mutual plan from those days of yesteryear, Dennis had also flown jets after graduation from the Naval Academy before the transition into NASA. He had been on one previous space shuttle flight as a mission specialist, and Ross knew Dennis had the qualifications necessary for this specific mission.

Soon after the intent of returning to the Moon had been divulged to Ross, he began to lobby for Dennis. NASA wanted to have Ross land the space shuttle on the Moon near the axis that defined the near and far side. Although the Moon orbits the Earth, it has no rotation of its own. The same side or half of the Moon, where all the previous Apollo missions had landed, always faces the Earth. It never changes, so nothing was currently known about the outward half other than the brief glimpses from above as the Apollo missions orbited the surface. The new intent was to establish a base at that axis point and explore, via rover vehicle and walking large sections of, the outward half of the Moon's surface.  That would include collecting deep core samples of the rock strata to determine where follow-up missions could safely build a permanent structure for a lunar base.  Ross knew of the multi-generational mining background that Dennis had, and that he excelled in the field of geology, so he seemed like the perfect fit.

NASA, like most other big business, needs to know how to play the media in the proper way.  The shuttle program was going well, but it would only be a matter of time before some people started to ask questions about why a certain shuttle wasn't being used for any of the multiple flights now scheduled each year.

The unveiling of the big news came at the perfect time.  The national economy was back on solid ground, so there was less concern about cutting the space program budget, and ambition was once again at the forefront of people's thoughts.  In May of 1985 NASA revealed to America, and the rest of the world, of their intent to return to the Moon with a manned space flight.   Some details of the modified space shuttle Discovery were given to the press, and they ran with it like wildfire.  NASA didn't have to spend a dime on publicity; they just let the world media do it for them.

Patty excitedly watched the news on the television, and couldn't wait to discuss it with Ross when he came home that evening, but she soon discovered that conversation would take on a different angle.  After showing photos of the newly revamped shuttle, the cameras within the NASA briefing room in Houston came to life.  Patty dropped her glass of ice tea and put her hands over her mouth, as her husband Ross and their old friend Dennis were introduced to the world as the crew of the upcoming mission. Her excitement gave way to a moment of anger as Ross had never mentioned any of this to her, but that was soon replaced by forgiveness as the senior NASA administrator informed the world that the Moon mission had been kept a secret intentionally.

Within minutes the phone began ringing off the hook, as wives of other astronauts called to make sure Patty was watching. That was followed by knocks on the door and hugs from some of her close friends, as the entire world seemed to know within hours of the announcement. Patty even received a call from her old friend and maid of honor Betty Collina, who was still living in the Washington D.C. area with her husband and young son.

When Ross finally made it home from work that evening, the girls met him at the door. As usual he gave them each a big hug, and picked them both up as he smiled in the direction of Patty. She returned the smile as he walked towards her, and then gave him a kiss before he put the girls down. Ross said he was sorry that she had to find out that way, but he had been ordered to not tell anyone. There was even a faction of people at NASA that didn't know about the planned mission, because there was concern about a potential security breech.

Luckily for Ross and Dennis, the majority of their necessary training had already taken place during the previous eighteen months. It seemed that everybody wanted a piece of them, and NASA knew how to ride the wave of popularity by making the two astronauts available for publicity events whenever possible. In the midst of all the ensuing chaos that occurred during the subsequent months, Ross had to explain to his daughter Aurora that he would have to miss her eighth birthday party in November. She didn't take the news well, but he promised to make it up to her by taking her wherever she wanted to go when he returned from the Moon. Although that promise gave her temporary comfort and stopped her tears, Aurora also made him promise to never miss another one of her birthdays because he was flying in space. Ross thought about her terms for a moment, realized the chances of him going on a subsequent mission in November were scarce at best, and reached out to shake her hand to seal the deal.

Soon the time had arrived for the final press briefing before the launch, and this one had considerably more members of the media in attendance. Ross had never seen the room so full of cameras and microphones, but he once again took it in stride by saying that it was wrong to place the two astronauts in the spotlight while literally thousands of people had worked very hard to make this mission to the Moon a reality. He and Dennis expertly navigated their way through the maze of questions whose answers dictated political correctness, and somehow tried to explain to the media how they couldn't possibly know how it would feel to walk on the Moon until they were actually there. In time a NASA administrator stepped in to field the ever increasing level of ridiculous questions, while Ross and Dennis were swept away into a secure location.

Later that day the two of them arrived on the Florida coastline for a few final days of training away from the eyes and ears of the media, and during that time they had a special visitor. President Ronald Reagan had come down from Washington D.C. in as quiet a manner as was possible for the leader of the free world, so that he could meet with the two astronauts privately. Ross and Dennis were both still active members of the military, so they snapped to attention as their Commander and Chief entered the room. A senior NASA administrator then introduced the two men who would be going on the historic flight by saying, "Mr. President may I present Commander Ross Martin of the United States Navy and Lieutenant Dennis Strickland of the United States Navy." There were no members of the media in attendance, and only a handful of secret service and high ranking NASA administrators were present as he motioned for Ross and Dennis to sit down before conversing with them for roughly thirty minutes.

When he rose to leave the room the two astronauts snapped to attention once again, and received the greatest gift of all as the President of the United States said "I should be the one saluting the two of you for what you are about to do for this country and mankind!" With that, the President shook their hands and left the room with the secret service in tow.

As had become his customary habit, on the morning of this long anticipated launch Ross rubbed the emblem on his necklace with his bare fingers one more time before being helped into his spacesuit. The crowds at the launch viewing points were larger than during some of the more recent missions, because some of those were perceived as routine by the public. Ross, and everyone at NASA for that matter, knew that all of those previous missions served as an important cog in the grand plan of space exploration, but this mission had the added significance of returning to the Moon.

The giant digital clock on the grounds near mission control that signified the countdown sequence moved within minutes of the launch, and the excitement level of the crowd began to rise. As if cheering on their favorite team in the closing seconds of a closely fought game, the crowd joined in unison with the voice over the loudspeaker and counted backwards from ten to one.

The mighty rockets came to life with a blast of smoke and fire, and the shuttle Discovery began to slowly pull away from the launch platform. Patty and Jessica, now witnessing their third launch, comforted Aurora and Rachel who were a bit scared by all the loud noise and commotion. Thousands of other spectators who had lined various viewing points on or near the grounds of the Kennedy Space Center tipped their heads backwards as the shuttle began to pick up speed and move skyward.

Ross and Dennis had a slightly bumpier ride than either had experienced on previous flights, but they thought that was probably due to the different configuration of the payload. The external main fuel tank and twin reusable rocket boosters that would soon be jettisoned had the same specifications as previous flights, but the shuttle itself had been reconfigured for this mission. Within the large cargo bay at the back end of the shuttle was the added weight of fuel tanks for the extended flight to the Moon, along with some minor building materials and machinery such as the rover vehicle for use on the surface. The plan was for much of this cargo, including the rover, to be left near the landing site on the Moon for use during future missions. If all went well with this three week mission, the next wave would bring additional components to begin assembling a livable habitat for longer durations on the surface.

Soon the ride smoothed out considerably as they escaped the confines of Earth's atmosphere, so Ross and Dennis went to work preparing for the next phase of the flight. It would only take them a few hours to orbit the Earth once, and then they would break away from orbit and set a course for the Moon.

With all systems ready to go, Ross awaited the instructions from mission control to begin the maneuver. At the appropriate time he pushed the correct buttons that would create the added boost to break orbit, and they were on their way. The burn of the engines would need to be about two minutes in length to attain the proper speed and course for the upcoming three day glide, so Ross decided he and Dennis should make good use of the time. With the aid of a harmonica that Dennis had smuggled aboard, the two astronauts began singing their own horrible rendition of Bart Howards "Fly Me to the Moon." Neither one of the two astronauts could sing very well, but they gave it their best effort as the song was now part of NASA's official transcript of the mission.

# 16

## The landing

The thrusters had fired perfectly to slow down the approaching shuttle Discovery, and she fell into a gentle orbit around the Moon. Ross and Dennis then began preparing for the upcoming landing. They had little time to work with, as the shuttle would make three orbits of the Moon while the thrusters occasionally fired to continue slowing the vessel, and then they would take it into a landing pattern.

Like all of her sister shuttles in the fleet, the Discovery was designed to land like an aircraft back on Earth. The same concept would be used by Ross for this landing on the Moon, but there were a few hugely significant differences in how he would approach each of the two landings during the mission. For a landing on Earth, the shuttle would come in fast and hard towards a lengthy runway, and there would be no opportunity for a second chance via a flyby. On the Moon, Ross had one-sixth of the gravity to contend with, less speed, and no runway. If absolutely necessary the thrusters could be used to create enough lift for a flyby, and then Ross could realign the shuttle for another landing attempt. He would land the Discovery on specially fitted skis that would later be jettisoned, but there would be very little roll out according to NASA's expectations.

The three day flight up to the Moon had been a smooth one, without even the smallest "glitch" that had been the well documented norm for the earlier missions of the Mercury, Gemini, and Apollo programs. The shuttle program had taken over the modern day of space flight, and this was the first of those vehicles to be used for a trip beyond a standard low Earth orbit. Several more missions were being scheduled to follow in the upcoming months and years, so the overall success of this particular mission added some weight to the two men chosen for the task at hand.

Ross brought the shuttle in on final approach over the chosen landing site, and touched it down on the relatively smooth surface well away from any deep craters. After checking all the systems for any problems, he and Dennis prepared to exit the craft onto the surface of the Moon.

Unlike the previous Apollo missions to have landed, the shuttle didn't have a fixed ladder on the side of the spacecraft for a relatively easy descent. The space shuttle had always been used for orbital missions that on occasion had docked with another vehicle in space, but when they returned to earth the astronauts used a slide from a blown hatch to exit the craft. It was another aspect of the retrofit that needed to be considered because the aforementioned section of each Apollo spacecraft had always been left on the lunar surface, while this entire vehicle would be returning to Earth. The engineers at NASA had finally decided that the best approach would be to store a ladder in the cargo bay with all the other equipment, and then mount it on the side of the shuttle for descent after the cargo bay doors had been opened. It was basically a glorified version of a ladder that would be placed on the side of a boat for water-skiers or swimmers to use, and was light enough that the large robotic arm used for other aspects of their cargo would not be needed.

The airlock connecting the crew cabin and flight deck to the cargo bay hissed open, and Ross stepped outside. With

Dennis close behind, the two of them moved the ladder into the proper position for Ross to make his historic descent. Dennis leaned out over the edge of the cargo bay with a hand held camera recording every move that Ross made. He did his best to keep steady, as this clip of film was being broadcast to every part of the Earth that had the technology to receive it. When Ross reached the bottom step, he looked back up at Dennis and waved to the camera. His words would not be the same as famously spoken by Neil Armstrong, but he knew they would go into the history books.

Ross spoke to the world when he said "Mankind has returned to the Moon as another step in our quest for knowledge through peaceful space exploration." With that Ross turned his gaze towards the ground below him, and pushed away from the ladder. A small amount of lunar dust was displaced by his boots after the fall of little more than a foot, and he was now standing on the surface of the Moon waiting for Dennis to join him.

# 17

## The lunar surface

Continuing the exploration patterns set forth by their superiors at NASA, astronauts Martin and Strickland began the tenth day of gathering and reporting data from the lunar surface. When they landed on Monday the 11th of November 1985 they had become the first humans to set foot on the Moon since the crew of Apollo 17 nearly thirteen years prior, but they had now exceeded the duration of that, or any other previous crews, time on the lunar surface by several days. As only the thirteenth and fourteenth persons to actually land, Ross and Dennis had become heroes back on Earth before they even returned from the mission.

After spending the entire first day taking promotional photographs for NASA and unloading the gear from the cargo bay, Ross and Dennis were then able to get busy with the more important task of exploration. Throughout the course of the first week of rover vehicle and walking patrols, there was nothing unusual or significant to report. The plan set forth by NASA was to begin a cautious exploration of the far side of the Moon from positions along the edge of the surface that always faces Earth. Because the plan was to continue this exploration for fourteen days, some of the terrain they needed to cover would be in darkness.

A typical cycle between full moons is a fraction over twenty-seven days, so it takes almost fourteen days for the Moon to visually change from full to a tiny crescent back on Earth. The same side of the Moon always faces the Earth, so areas of light and dark upon the Moon change just as they do on Earth. When a crescent is viewed, the far side is almost entirely illuminated by the sun, but when a full moon is viewed that same surface area is in total darkness.

Their first eight days on the surface had been in sunlight, but now the Moon had rotated far enough around the Earth that the remainder of their time would be in the darkness. According to the expectations of NASA, the sun would rise again just before their planned departure and voyage back to Earth. Exploration in sunlight was easier because the solar powered rover could move about with relative ease and cover more ground each day, but their exploration technique had changed due to the total darkness that had engulfed them. The batteries of the rover could last with minimal driving for a day, but would need to be recharged by a power source back at the shuttle at the conclusion of each day's work.

The rover would be driven out in a straight line to a designated spot each day, and turned around to face the tire tracks it had made in the lunar dust before Ross and Dennis would begin their exploration. All the lights and panels on the rover would then be turned off to save power except for one light at the top of the antenna assembly.

Using two spooled tethers mounted on opposite ends of the vehicle, each astronaut would clip a tether to their spacesuits before walking in opposite directions until the two hundred meters of length upon each spool was completely unwound. At that point they would each turn ninety degrees to face the same direction, and venture on while keeping the tether as taunt as possible until coming face to face at the conclusion of their respective ninety degree sweeps. They would then walk in tandem following a fairly straight course back to the rover before recording their findings and performing the same ritual on the other side of the rover. As had been the plan, five of these circles had been completed every day, including the first day of darkness, without any problems. Ross and Dennis had always easily found their way back to the rover with the help of the light at the top of the antenna, and the headlamps on their spacesuits lit up the area immediately around them quite well.

Satisfied with their progress during the first day of total darkness, the powers that be back at NASA had instructed the two man crew of the Discovery to proceed with the original plan for six more days of the same exploration pattern. In some regard that overjoyed Ross and Dennis, as continued exploration of the so called "new frontier" of the far, and now dark, side would undoubtedly guarantee them a place in the history books. In essence, their mission was nearly the equivalent of Apollo 11 that had brought former astronauts Neil Armstrong and Buzz Aldrin to the first exploration of this desolate rock in space. The down side to six more days of the same semi-circle explorations was that both men had hoped for more excitement while on the Moon, and the search patterns and core samples of the previous eight days had yielded nothing that would fit into that category.

At the conclusion of each day's walk on the surface, Ross had acted as the lab assistant by moving around core samples and inputting the results of tests performed by Dennis into the computer for further analysis. While in the makeshift lab aboard the space shuttle, Dennis had recorded some data of rock structure that would be suitable for a solid foundation on which to build a future habitat and lab. Their recommendations would be taken into account, but the boys back at NASA would have the final say on the validity of their findings.

As Ross brought the rover vehicle to a stop where he and Dennis would begin their third sweep of the day, they each commented on their desire to record finding something other than more rocks. Regardless of that sentiment, as commander of the mission Ross reminded his good friend that they needed to stay focused on the task at hand. Their speech needed to be somewhat selective, as every word spoken by them during their explorations could become part of the official record.

A few minutes later, in what he guessed to be about halfway through his sweep, the tether for Ross snagged on a rock. That in itself was nothing new, as a similar event had occurred during at least half of the previous sweeps. This time however, something different caught his eye. As Ross turned to shake the bright orange tether free from the surface rock, something on top of the Moon dust glistened in response to his spacesuit headlamp. He swiveled his head back to see the glimmer again, and then began to move towards it as he created slack in the tether.

Reaching the location of the shiny object, Ross lowered himself to one knee and removed it from the thin layer of moon dust. When he opened his gloved hand to gaze upon the object, everything his grandfather Hank had ever told him about the crash site of 1897 became instantly verified. He could hardly believe his eyes, as he was staring at an identical emblem to the one that Grandpa Hank had passed down to him. At four to five inches in length it was significantly larger than the one on the necklace that he had cherished all those years, but it was most definitely the same emblem. A shout of, "Oh my God" brought forth a reaction from Dennis, who at that moment was going through the paces of another uneventful sweep. Dennis asked him what he had seen, but Ross knew he couldn't tell him because the response would become part of the official transcripts. He decided instead to report that he was just taken aback by all the additional stars visible from their current position on the dark side.

As Ross began to regain his wits, and wrap his brain around the significance and complexity of his discovery, things suddenly became even more intense. With artifact in hand, he stood to resume his search pattern. He thought to himself that nothing else he might find on this sweep would compare to the emblem still clutched in his hand, but that could not have been further from the truth. Ross came to an abrupt halt when his headlamp suddenly revealed something about twenty meters in front of him. It became abundantly clear that something else was searching for what he held in his hand, and that something was staring right at him.

Like Columbus encountering the natives of the "new world", Commander Ross Martin was involved in a first contact situation. The significance of this encounter however, was that the contact was with a life form not of Earthly origin. The alien life form took a few steps forward, and Ross' natural reaction was to step back in an attempt to maintain the distance between them. That caused the alien life form to stop the advance, so Ross relaxed somewhat and halted his retreat. A few seconds later Ross took a deeper than usual breath before beginning his own cautious advance, and the alien life form held its ground. After about five steps Ross stopped and motioned with his hand for the alien life form to move forward. This time Ross did not retreat when the alien life form advanced, and the two of them then took turns moving closer to one another until Ross could tell the alien was only about four feet tall. He also noticed that the alien had no real spacesuit to speak of, but was using some sort of breathing apparatus that bore the same emblem Ross had held dear for so many years. The alien also wore a thin layer of some sort of clothing with a few different emblems on it, but it did not cover the head, hands, or feet of the occupant.

In an instant of total clarity, he knew what had to be done. In perhaps the most significant act of diplomacy ever displayed by a human being, Commander Ross Martin reached out with trembling open hand and offered the shiny emblem to its rightful owner. The alien reached for the object with what resembled a hand of three very long skinny fingers and a thumb, then with a nod of acknowledgement retrieved it.

Ross turned to head towards the rover vehicle while motioning for the alien to follow. Without ever moving its mouth, the alien began to communicate with Ross. Although he couldn't understand at that time how he could hear the aliens thoughts, Ross could hear them just the same. He then turned off his voice recorder so he could safely verbalize to the alien creature that he wanted to show him something back at the rover.

Several weeks before the launch, Ross had asked some of the technicians if they could do him a favor. He had a copy of the emblem on his necklace fabricated and put on a strong chain, and his plan was to have it hang on the rearview mirror of the rover while he and Dennis were driving it on the surface of the Moon for fourteen days.  Knowing that the mission needed a bit of stealthy levity, and understanding that a pair of fuzzy dice was somehow inappropriate, they had complied with his request.  The technicians had smuggled the trinket aboard just hours before the launch, and had informed Ross and Dennis where they could find it once they landed on the Moon.

A few times during the walk back to the rover, Ross looked over his shoulder to make sure the alien was still following him.  The alien was keeping a safe distance and would stop briefly every time Ross turned around, but he was still there.  Suddenly a shout of panic from Dennis came over the intercom, and Ross had a decision to make.  He could see the small light at the top of the rovers' antenna as he was now less than fifty meters away from it, but Dennis was in some sort of trouble.  Ross made the only decision that he could by turning left towards the area where Dennis would be.  He located the bright orange tether that was clipped onto Dennis and followed it away from the rover.  What he saw a moment later was shocking to say the least, as two bodies lay flat on the lunar surface.  Ross moved past the first body, which was the second alien life form he had seen in the last fifteen minutes, and some twenty meters later arrived at the side of Dennis.

After a quick look at his friend's spacesuit, Ross knew there was nothing he could do.  Dennis only had a few minutes of life left in him, as the tear in his spacesuit and badly cracked face shield on his helmet were both venting his oxygen into space.  The suit was depressurizing, and soon the environment inside would not support human life.

Meanwhile the alien that Ross had made contact with had arrived at the body of his friend to determine the extent of his injuries. Ross looked over at the two aliens for a few seconds when he heard the voice in his head informing him of their situation. The injuries to the second alien were minimal and not life threatening, but there was damage to his breathing apparatus that would need attention sooner than later if he was to survive. Ross then reached down to disconnect the voice recorder on his old friend's spacesuit, and informed him that he could speak freely about his current thoughts because it would not become part of the official transcript. He then asked Dennis, "What happened?" as he placed his hand over the large tear near the tether clip in an attempt to slow down the venting process.

Dennis said, "I was startled when I first saw the alien creature and attempted to move away, but that's when all hell broke loose!" His bright orange tether attached to the rover was caught on a rock, and when he finally won the struggle to break it free there was a large amount of slack in the line. Dennis stumbled backwards while trying to regain his balance and the tether whipped across the legs of the alien who was approaching. That caused the creature to be knocked off his feet and land poorly on his breathing apparatus. That action threw Dennis more off balance and he spun face first into a large rock that he would tumble wildly over. His face shield cracked from the sudden impact, and there wasn't enough slack left in the tether line for his final tumble to the ground. That's how the large tear was created in his spacesuit, and the cause for his shout of panic.

Ross informed Dennis that he had met the other of the two aliens, and propped his old friend up against the rock so he could see them both some twenty meters away. Dennis could hardly believe his eyes as he looked at the two alien creatures through his badly cracked face shield, but was also unable to take his eyes off of them. Ross informed Dennis that he didn't know how he could hear their thoughts directed at him, but there had been some communication between the two species before Dennis had his own contact.

The two old friends knew that Dennis only had a few minutes left, but at least whatever each one of them had to say would not be recorded for all of mankind to dissect. As a final act of duty and friendship, Ross made a promise to Dennis that he would get him back to Earth aboard the Discovery and deliver any last message he might have to his parents or other family members.

A few minutes later Dennis was dead, and the alien creature was standing in front of Ross communicating with him again. An expression of sorrow for the loss of Dennis was conveyed to Ross by the alien, and then the creature asked Ross for some help. They needed to join forces and figure out a way to fix the other aliens breathing apparatus, or he would suffer the same fate as Dennis in the not too distant future.

By using a small piece of the human spacesuit worn by Dennis, they could repair the problem with the aliens breathing apparatus. Dennis obviously wouldn't need it anymore, so the two new friends from different worlds worked together in a magnificent example of interstellar cooperation.

The next daunting task for Ross would be to explain to NASA what had happened, and get Dennis back on board the space shuttle for the eventual return to Earth. Mission control would already be aware of some level of problem, as the monitors showing both astronauts' vital signs would be reading all flat lines for Dennis. That would mean that the sensors in his spacesuit had either malfunctioned, or he was indeed dead, but they would have to wait for Ross to communicate with them to verify either scenario. Ross knew that he would have to finish his business with the alien creatures before communicating with Earth, so he resumed his original course of action by having the aliens follow him back to the rover.

Upon their arrival, Ross showed them both the emblem floating upwards from the chain around the rearview mirror of the rover. It was a copy of the one that Ross had found a short time ago on the surface, but the aliens were surprised to see a rendition of the emblem that was on their breathing apparatus.

The next several minutes involved Ross hearing both questions and answers in his mind, although he could never see either one of the aliens' mouths moving. He learned that the aliens had a small observation base on what humans referred to as the far side of the Moon, and that it had either never been detected by any of the Apollo missions that had previously orbited the Moon, or the astronauts simply feared the repercussions of reporting such findings.

Ross also learned that the alien species had been visiting Earth, along with several other planets within the solar system, for more than two hundred cycles of our planets rotation around the host star. As the closest planet to the star that also had a moon, they had used this planets orbit to determine a time line of their current observations. Ross quickly converted that into Earth years of over two centuries, and then he asked them what they called his planet. The two aliens informed him everything was labeled via a system of symbols and numbers, because that was after all the universal language. This particular solar system was known on the home world as number ₹-829 of the systems their species had charted. Each planet in each solar system was then classified by other aspects if it contained life and numbered according to its order from the host star, thus Ross' home world was known as ₹-829-ᴣᴫ-3 to the aliens. They asked him what the planet was called by the inhabitants, and Ross informed them it was known by the humans as Earth.

It was obvious to Ross from this encounter that the alien species was far more advanced than humans from a technological standpoint, but they were still vulnerable as life forms to different atmospheric conditions. He asked the alien creatures how many planetary systems their species had charted, and to what extent humans rated with relation to other life forms they had encountered.

His new friends informed Ross that their species had traveled to and charted slightly over one thousand solar systems in this particular section of the galaxy alone, but had found life of some sort in only about twenty percent of those systems. It was an ongoing process for their species to try and communicate with life forms that they thought were ready both philosophically, and technologically, for the encounter. They also informed Ross that the two of them had actually only been to a few dozen of that large number of systems, and their current observation assignment had them rotating between this and three other nearby solar systems.

According to the archives, many of the life forms that had been discovered were not yet ready for such contact, while others had developed to the point of searching the stars themselves for other inhabitants. In that regard they classified

₹-829-૩π-3, or Earth as they now knew it to be called, as an emerging planet whose dominant species could be ready for contact.  During their most current observations of the past few centuries, the aliens had witnessed some significant progress on the planet from a technological standpoint.  They also had major concerns about the mental and philosophical element of human evolution, because of the seemingly endless need for killing each other, and the destruction of natural resources.

That new found information explained several things to Ross, such as the emblem on his grandfather Hank's necklace that Ross had cherished for many years.  Hank had received the gift from his father when he was only four years old in 1897, and it supposedly came from the crash site of a flying machine of some sort.

When Ross informed the aliens of the necklace that he currently wore, which was the prototype of the emblem on the rover, they conveyed to him that it was indeed from one of their crashed scout vehicles.  What was also intriguing to Ross was that by the aliens' calendar that crash in western Texas had occurred less than four months ago.  That meant that one of their months was approximately equal to twenty-five years on Earth.

At the conclusion of their educational discussion, the two aliens helped Ross bring the dead body of Dennis back to the rover before they returned to their base.  Ross had removed the heavy and cumbersome breathing pack from the body before doing so, as it was both no longer needed by Dennis, and the missing piece would be challenging for Ross to explain back on Earth.  Ross then assured the aliens that he would not report their existence to his superiors back on Earth, but that future scheduled missions to the Moon could detect their base. If that were to happen, Ross couldn't guarantee that those astronauts would also remain silent.

The two aliens had seen so many acts of kindness from Ross over the past few Earth hours that they believed his statement. They informed Ross that they hoped future contact with him would be possible, but didn't really think it was probable. If future contact could be made, they would attempt to do it in a discreet way to protect Ross. With that they shook hands, bid farewell, and Ross climbed into the rover.

His new friends walked away and disappeared into the darkness, while Ross sat in reflective silence for several minutes before turning his voice recorder back on. It had been one hell of a few hours to say the least, as he had encountered an alien species from a distant world, watched his good friend and fellow astronaut Dennis die, and then formed a friendship with the aliens who were indirectly responsible for his death. Ross turned to see his dead friend in the second seat of the rover, and then began the powering up procedure so he could return to the shuttle and communicate with mission control.

# 18

## The lonely ride home

The news Ross delivered to mission control had been shocking. Astronaut Dennis Strickland was dead due to an accident while conducting a normal survey exploration on the surface of the Moon. Ross had explained that he had heard a cry for help in a moment of panic, which was confirmed by the voice recorder, and that he immediately made his way towards Dennis. Unfortunately by the time he got to his side there was nothing that could be done, and Ross had made the decision to turn off each of their voice recorders so the painful death of his friend would not be heard and dissected by the entire world.

When asked why he had not turned back on his own voice recorder after Dennis had died, Ross explained that there was nothing to say at that time and he was more focused on figuring out a way to get his friend's body back to the rover. In spite of the lessor gravity, it took a great amount of time and effort to move Dennis the required distance. During that process Ross had determined that he needed to remove the backpack from his friend's suit to lessen the weight of the lifeless body. That was a boldface lie he was telling NASA, but the chances of them finding out the truth were minimal at best. Ross had been helped with moving the body, and the pack with a now missing part needed to be left on the surface. His story was plausible, and would explain the time lapse that had been used in quiet contemplation back at the rover.

After several minutes of waiting for instructions from NASA, Ross was informed that the overall length of the mission would be cut short. He had suspected that would be the course of action due to what had taken place, but he wasn't happy with the decision. Privately he knew that this was a tremendous opportunity to communicate with the alien species at greater length, but he couldn't tell NASA that was why he wanted to stay for the remaining scheduled days. Ross was instructed to get the dead body of Dennis aboard the shuttle by any means possible, even if that meant using the robotic arm normally reserved for cargo. Ross then lost his cool for a moment when he sharply informed NASA that, "I fully intend to bring Dennis back to Earth, but I will attempt to find a more humane way to get the body back on board the Discovery!"

Ross climbed the ladder leading into the cargo bay, and ran one of the tethers attached to the rover around the top rung. He then tied and clipped it around the chest area of Dennis before slowly moving the rover away from the shuttle to pull the body across a few feet of the lunar surface and up the ladder. Ross climbed the ladder with the other tether that he had disconnected from the rover, and tied it around the legs of the lifeless body. It was difficult for Ross to get past the body with limited space on the ladder, but he was on a mission and determined to climb inside the cargo bay. He then wrapped the tether attached to the legs around a harness, and used it as a pulley system to lift the majority of Dennis' body over the lip of the cargo bay. After unclipping and tossing away the first tether, Ross then lowered the body as gently as possible down into the cargo bay.

With the most significant aspect of the challenge behind him, Ross now only needed to move the body along the floor of the cargo bay towards the hatch. He pulled Dennis into the airlock area, shut the door, and heard the hissing sound of the compartment being pressurized with oxygen. Once inside the shuttles flight deck and living area, he placed Dennis in a bunk and strapped the body down with the bright orange tether.

He returned briefly to the surface of the Moon to power down the rover and stow away any loose equipment. As had been the plan from the beginning, the pole holding the American flag was then lashed to the rover with the remaining tether so it would never fall down, and Ross climbed back up the ladder into the cargo bay. He saluted the flag and flung the ladder away from the ship before returning to the airlock. With the cargo bay doors closed, he got out of his spacesuit to get some much needed sleep before the flight back to Earth.

The next morning, at the direction of mission control, Ross began the launch sequence. He would need to do the work of two men, so the pre-flight sequencing took a little longer than usual. Soon the shuttle Discovery was ready to go for the first ever horizontal liftoff by any of the five in the current fleet. The engines roared to life, and moon dust shot out from behind the vehicle as it moved forward on the wheels and skis below.

Little did Ross know that the entire operation was being viewed from a distance, as his new alien friends had come to see the spectacle. With only one-sixth the gravity of Earth, the shuttle rose easily from the surface of the Moon. Per the flight plan Ross gained altitude slowly until reaching a safe height, jettisoned the skies, retracted the landing gear, and put the shuttle into orbit around the Moon. He then increased speed with a continued engine burn while orbiting a half dozen times before the three day return trip to Earth.

# 19

## The cape

The shuttle Discovery glowed in the fiery intensity of re-entry into the Earth's atmosphere, as Ross handled the controls during the bumpy ride. He was having as much fun with the flight as in previous missions, but this time there was no one to share the joy with. He glanced over at the chair where Dennis should have been seated, and said into the microphone that he was missing a great ride. The ship was currently in a time of communication blackout with mission control due to the ionization build up caused during re-entry, so they didn't hear what Ross had said. That didn't matter though, because it would be recorded in the official transcript.

Ross had looked over at the empty chair probably dozens of times during the three day return trip from the Moon, and visited the body strapped onto a bunk a few times as well. It had been a lonely three days with only the occasional communication with mission control back home to break up the solitude, but it was almost over. He wondered if anyone on Earth other than NASA was aware of what had happened to Dennis. They would inherently want to keep the mishap from the public, but news of this magnitude would be difficult to keep from leaking out somehow.

Soon those waiting for the landing in Florida would hear the twin sonic booms created by the shuttle informing them that the time was near. Ross performed a series of turns to help spill off some speed, and the guidance computer helped him line up with the new runway at Cape Canaveral. In the early days of the shuttle program all landings had been at Edwards Air Force Base in California, with one landing at White Sands in New Mexico due to poor weather conditions over the California site, but NASA had now built a long enough runway adjacent to the launch facility in Florida.

Ross brought the Discovery down to a smooth textbook landing, and at "wheels stop" spoke his customary "What a fun ride" into the microphone before signing off. Many had doubted that he could bring the shuttle safely back to Earth, but were glad to hear that in spite of the added pressure of a solo landing, he still maintained a certain amount of levity. As the commander of the flight, Ross refused to leave the ship until Dennis had been properly removed, so a platform was brought up next to the escape hatch of the Discovery. Four technicians that Ross knew well from pre-launch then came aboard with a gurney to remove the body, and took turns shaking Ross' hand.

Unafraid of any repercussions or interpretations by NASA or the media, Ross stood at attention by the escape hatch and saluted his old friend and fellow astronaut as he was rolled onto the awaiting platform. Only after the body of Dennis was safely at ground level did Ross disembark the Discovery and begin the walk towards the awaiting recovery vehicles.

The debriefing was of course much different than his two previous flights into space, and the media was everywhere. Ross now had an answer to his internal question of a few minutes before, as it was obvious that the news about the accident on the Moon had gotten out somehow. Ross felt bad about not being able to field all the questions from the media straight away, but there was information about the mission that Ross couldn't tell them until cleared to do so by his superiors.

He also knew that there was some information that he probably couldn't ever reveal.

Before he would ever get an opportunity to field the inevitable multitude of questions from the national and world media, Ross knew that he would have to deal with a barrage of questions from the NASA administrators. The mission had been going so well up to the point of the accident that killed Dennis, and from a technical standpoint everything had been perfect.

The launch and Earth orbit, the three day glide to the Moon, the engine burn to slow the spacecraft down for orbit and subsequent landing on the Moon had all gone exactly as planned. The two astronauts had unloaded the gear from the space shuttle's cargo bay and spent more than eight days exploring, collecting core samples and surface rocks, and recording the data in the small lab aboard the ship without any problems whatsoever. In spite of that, to some the mission would be considered a failure due to the loss of one life. Even the return "never been done before" horizontal launch from the Moon, assent to orbit, three day glide back to Earth, and a successful landing at Cape Canaveral had gone better than ever hoped for because those aspects of the mission had been done single handedly by Ross.

Much to their credit, NASA stood up for Ross by pointing out all those positive aspects of the mission when a few members of the media attempted to put a negative spin on things. It soon occurred to Ross that in the eyes of NASA he was a hero for bringing back the space shuttle in one piece and proving that establishing a permanent base on the surface of the Moon was possible. Was it dangerous? Of course it was, but all exploration and scientific advancement was inherently dangerous and the envelope had to be pushed if mankind was to advance. When all was said and done, it was comforting for Ross to know that NASA had his back.

Even though it had only been a few hours since Ross had landed the Discovery, it seemed like forever before he was done with the initial debriefing. He wanted to see Patty and the girls who were waiting for him in another building nearby, and each minute that passed before he could hug them all was pure torture to him at this point. When Ross strolled down the hall to the family waiting room with a lone NASA representative by his side, his thoughts once again moved to Dennis. His parents were supposed to be in the room as well for the reunion, and he wondered how that had been handled by NASA.

His escort opened the door for him, and waited outside while Ross reconnected with his family. The girls had run over to him in their customary fashion, while Patty stood motionless fighting back the tears. Ross picked up the girls and carried them over to his wife, then set them down to receive a long awaited embrace. Patty fell into his arms and kissed him as her tears began to flow. Then she said, "I would really appreciate it if you would promise me that you will never venture into space again." To which Ross said, "Based on what happened to Dennis, NASA may have already made that decision for me, but I can't promise you that I won't go back into space again if the opportunity presents itself!"

After a private thirty minutes of telling the girls and Patty all about, well mostly all about, his adventure on the Moon, a knock on the door informed them that a vehicle was in place to take them all away from the media circus outside. Ross knew there would be a more complete media intrusion with all their questions in the future, but he was glad it was over for the day. Before they departed Patty informed Ross that her mother Elizabeth had flown down to Cape Canaveral with them, and had agreed to take the girls out for pizza and keep them overnight. Patty's plan was to have some alone time with Ross, and he smiled broadly when she winked at him and said, "It's not every day a girl gets to make love to a man who has walked on the Moon!"

Later that night after a recovery nap, Patty informed Ross of the other news that had occurred in the last few days. She wanted to keep it from him until after they had their time alone, because she knew it would shake him up considerably. She told him that his father Robert had taken ill, and Jessica had informed Patty that the doctors didn't think he had much longer to live. Jessica was already by his side in the Army hospital at Fort Hood, and Patty, with the help of NASA, had arranged for Ross to fly out there in the morning. Patty, along with the girls and her mother Elizabeth, would fly back to Houston and wait for Ross to contact them.

# 20

## Fort Hood, Texas

Ross entered the hospital room of his father, Lieutenant Colonel Robert Martin, and greeted his sister Jessica who had been by their father's side for three days. His familiar comment of, "Good to see you, and how does the leg feel?" made Jessica feel better instantly. The difficulty of their father's condition was also momentarily forgotten, as Ross gave his kid sister a hug and kissed her forehead like he had done so many times in the simpler days of yesteryear. She smiled and reported that she was doing well with the new brace, and then congratulated Ross on the success of his recent mission to the Moon. She also offered her heartfelt condolences for the loss of his longtime friend Dennis.

Many years before, Jessica had thought Dennis to be quite dashing, and had entertained the possibility of advancing upon him around the time of Ross and Patty's wedding. Luckily for all involved she had been too shy for the moment, and had since learned that those were the misgivings of a young girl of eighteen caught up in the favorable emotions of a wedding and a man in uniform. Never the less, now a well-educated woman who would soon be thirty-one, she knew Dennis Strickland to be a man of character that her brother Ross had trusted, so she was therefore pained by his death.

At that moment a few doctors and nurses came into the room and fired off a military salute to Commander Ross Martin out of respect for his rank and recent achievement. The news of his arrival had undoubtedly been reported by the nurse who

98

had informed him of what room his father Robert was in, and he hoped that the media hadn't been notified as well. Ross returned the salute before asking them to update him on his father's condition, while also requesting that the hospital staff refrain from such saluting action in the future and the media not be informed of his location on the base.

Without any level of "sugar coating" the doctors informed Ross of what they had told Jessica the previous day, and it wasn't good news. Robert had a fast moving form of cancer that was inoperable, and he had a week to live at best. It was Monday the 25th of November, and Thanksgiving was only three days away. Robert who had been sleeping soundly a few minutes before was now beginning to stir with the commotion of all the people in the room, so Ross and Jessica moved to his side. He smiled at the sight of his now fully grown children standing over him, and turned his head away briefly to gaze at a photograph on the bedside table. It had been many years since he last saw them both at the same time, but was relieved that he had the opportunity to do so.

After talking with their father for a few minutes before he nodded off to sleep again, Ross and Jessica ventured outside of the room into the hallway for a moment to converse with the doctors. They brought Ross further up to speed by informing him that although Robert now slept most of the time, they could keep him awake with medication if it was so desired. Ross and Jessica wanted Robert to remain as peaceful and pain free as possible during his final days, but liked the idea of medicating him to full consciousness should anyone in the family wish to have a final visit. They also gave the doctors all the latitude they needed to keep him alive beyond Thursday, because it would be a shame to have him pass away on Thanksgiving Day. Assured that the medical team would do their best, Ross headed for the pay phone down the hall to contact Patty with the news. If anyone wanted to see Robert one last time before his death, they had better make it quick.

Twenty minutes later Ross returned to the room to find Jessica at their father's side once again, and asked her to come back into the hall for a discussion. He informed Jessica that Patty and her mother Elizabeth would be arriving later that night with the girls, so she should go get some sleep and a shower before they all arrived. Patty and Ross had agreed that the drive up from Houston would be easier at night because the girls would sleep most of the way, and they knew that the whirlwind pace associated with the events of the last few days had already taken a toll on them. It was important that Aurora and Rachel make the trip because they had only seen their grandfather a handful of times during their short lives, and this would indeed be their last chance to see him.

The following morning the entire family arrived at Robert's hospital room to find Ross asleep in the corner chair. He had used his new found celebrity status to arrange for much more comfortable accommodations on base for the rest of the family, but he had wanted to stay by his father's side. Patty woke him with a kiss on the cheek before the girls rushed to his side, and Jessica thanked him for taking over her spot in the chair. She had spent the previous two nights in the same spot, so she knew all too well about how uncomfortable the night was that her brother had just endured.

As had been promised by the medical staff, Robert was soon fully awake with the assistance of some medication and ready to take on what the next few hours would entail. He had the opportunity to see both of his young grandchildren, which reminded him of when Ross and Jessica were that age. He instantly flashed back in his mind to the glorious times they all had before his wife Janet had been taken from him, but that was now over twenty-eight years in the past. After talking with the girls for several minutes and hearing them both giggle a few times, they were taken out into the hall so he could speak with each of the adults privately.

Patty was first in line, and Robert thanked her for her support of his sons' dreams to fly jets and become an astronaut. He knew that she had missed Ross very much when they were apart, and was well aware of the pain that one feels when their soul mate is absent. Next was his old neighbor and friend Elizabeth, and Robert was respectfully apologetic towards her. She had done so much throughout the many years before to help with the raising of both Ross and Jessica after Grandpa Hank had suddenly passed away, but he hadn't always recognized her for it. He also realized that Elizabeth had made gestures of wanting to perhaps take their relationship to a romantic level, but he had never fully been able to get over Janet and wouldn't walk down that path. Then of course there was his ongoing battle with the bottle, and he knew that she felt he had crawled inside it far too many times as the years went by. All those factors had made Robert somewhat of a "son of a bitch" in her eyes, but it was of great comfort to her that he had come clean and apologized to her in his final days.

When Ross and Jessica entered the room to conclude the visitation, Robert asked if he could see them both for a longer visit after everyone else had returned home. He had something that was very important to share with them, and he didn't want anyone else to possibly interrupt. They agreed to his conditions, but were somewhat puzzled by the request. Within an hour, all except Ross and Jessica were on their way back to nearby Rumley. The group of women had decided to try and make the most of a bad situation by throwing together a Thanksgiving meal at Elizabeth's house, but Robert's condition would have an impact on when, or if, the gathering would take place.

The doctors boosted the medication for Robert to keep him alert, posted a reliable sentry outside his door to prevent a disturbance, and informed Ross to let them know when he and Jessica had completed their private meeting with their father. With the room to themselves for however long was necessary, Ross and Jessica pulled up two chairs close to the bed to hear whatever Robert had to say. Jessica then removed a legal pad of paper from her backpack to take down any pertinent notes, and the session began.

In typical fashion for someone on their death bed, Robert listed all the things he had done incorrectly during his life, and what he would change if given the opportunity. He continued by adding how proud he was of both of them for their accomplishments, and how he intended to pass along the house and the few worldly possessions he owned to them and his grandchildren. At the conclusion of all the rhetoric that in no way needed a sentry outside the door for absolute privacy, the point of it all became clear when Robert began to tell Ross and Jessica the story of their mother Janet.

# 21

## The unparalleled secret

Robert began by asking Jessica to hand him the framed photograph from the bedside table. Both she and Ross knew the old black and white photograph well, as it had been at their father's bedside since they were children. It was snapped only a few weeks before the accident that had taken Janet from them all, and it showed the four of them sitting together on the front porch steps with smiling faces. Not sure how much, if anything at all, that Jessica had remembered about her mother, Robert told the story of how he and Janet had met.

The year was 1947, and the place was the small town of Roswell in the southeastern New Mexico desert. Janet was a nurse stationed at the Air Force base hospital, while Robert had been flown in from his nearby posting at Fort Bliss. He had been assigned as part of a crew that was tasked with cleaning up debris from a rather unusual situation. A craft of unknown origin had crashed on a ranch just outside of town, and keeping said crash a secret from the public was imperative during the early days of what would become a decade's long cold war between the United States and the Soviet Union.

During the first few days following the crash, Robert had the chance to meet Janet when he and his crew visited the base hospital for routine checkups. There had been some fear that the group of officers and enlisted men under Robert's command may have been exposed to radiation during the cleanup process, and Janet was a member of the medical team that administered the necessary tests and treatment. Janet was not at all disturbed by that course of action, or the need for it, as she had been a firsthand witness to some of the contents that had been removed from the crash site. She had caught a few brief glimpses of the bodies that had piloted the craft, and it seemed highly unlikely they were of Earthly origin.

Although both Robert and Janet had been sworn to secrecy about what they had seen or heard during the course of the investigation, they knew they could speak of the event privately between themselves. The magnitude of the discovery made it necessary to discuss it with someone, so they used the opportunity to get to know each other a little better. Their relationship continued to develop, and a little over a year after their first meeting they were married.

Everything was perfect in their lives. Bolstered by his stellar actions during World War II, Robert was enjoying a fast rise in the military ranks. He had enlisted shortly after the attack on Pearl Harbor in December of 1941, and before the wars end had been accepted into OCS, or Officers Candidate School. Once a commissioned officer, Robert continued to shine and had been promoted from Second Lieutenant to First Lieutenant before meeting Janet in 1947. His seemingly meteoric rise continued as he was promoted once again to Captain before Ross was born in July of 1950, and attained the rank of Major, like his father, before Jessica had come along in January of 1955. Due in part to her college education and training as a nurse, Janet had been commissioned as a Second Lieutenant in the Air Force and had been promoted once to First Lieutenant before resigning to raise the children.

Both Ross and Jessica had heard the story of how their parents had met a few times over the years, but they had not known about the supposed alien spacecraft, or the visual account their mother had of the occupants.  Robert informed them that both he and Janet would have been charged with, and most definitely found guilty of, treason against the United States had they ever spoken of what had taken place at Roswell.  None of that mattered anymore though, as Janet was gone and Robert had only days or hours to live.  The government couldn't hurt him anymore, but he cautioned Ross and Jessica to keep that information, and what was to come, from the outside world or they would probably face consequences that could hinder their careers and freedom.

Jessica informed Robert that she had a few fragmented memories of her mother, but had obviously remembered Grandpa Hank much more clearly.  That was only natural as Janet had died in the automobile accident when Jessica was only two years old, while Grandpa Hank had been a major influence during the next four years of her life before his death.  Ross chimed in by adding that he remembered several events with their mother, and had helped Jessica fill in the blanks whenever she had asked about her.

Robert smiled at the thought of those wonderful years when the four of them had enjoyed a good home life, and family picnics whenever possible.  It was then that he asked his two children if they remembered the white station wagon with a thick red stripe on each side.  It was the vehicle that Janet had frequently used for errands and such around town, and she took the children with her from time to time.  Ross nodded with a positive response to the question, but was saddened at the memory of that being the car she was also killed in.  He had never seen the wreckage of the car, but had always assumed his father had kept them away from it to lessen their pain. Robert then informed Ross and Jessica that the reason they had never seen the car again was because it had been taken away.

On what had been a rare opportunity for a summer overnight getaway without the children, Robert and Janet had arranged for the kids to stay with a family in town so they could enjoy a quiet celebration of ten years together. They had driven about twenty miles from home to a secluded location that had become one of their favorite spots throughout the years, and Robert parked the station wagon about one-hundred yards from where they would set up camp. From that spot they would have a nice view of a stand of old growth trees near the bend in a small creek that was an additional one-hundred yards away, and Janet felt strongly that it was possible Jessica had been conceived at that location.

Jessica blushed at hearing that news from her father and thanked him for telling her as she clasped his hand, but he was not yet finished with the story.

Robert continued by informing his children that it had been a beautiful afternoon, and the crystal clear night sky had provided the opportunity for some fantastic star gazing. He and Janet were enjoying a feeling of total freedom, and it had been wonderful to make love spontaneously a few times by the campfire without the risk of the children either hearing them or bursting into their bedroom unannounced.

To that comment Ross felt embarrassed, as he suddenly realized he had probably been guilty of that action a few times without knowing it when he was a small boy. He also felt he remembered the place that his father was speaking of, as he had probably been there with them a few times in his youth.

At some point during the course of the night Janet felt a chill and returned to the station wagon to retrieve some additional blankets, while Robert headed down towards the creek to get some water for the coffee pot. While he was there he moved behind one of the trees to relieve himself, and he never saw Janet again. With no warning of any kind, or sense of impending doom in the air, a huge cone shaped bright light suddenly appeared over the car and began to lift it skyward.

From his position near the creek roughly two-hundred yards away, Robert had no chance at all to prevent his wife's abduction. Janet and the red and white striped station wagon were taken upward very quickly, and by the time he covered the distance to its previous parking spot on the old dirt road it was at least twenty feet into the air. Robert yelled for Janet to jump out, but it was to no avail as she was somehow paralyzed by the light source. He could hear her desperately screaming for help as the car floated higher and higher, and he felt completely powerless as there was nothing he could do.

A few seconds later the source of the intensely bright lights swallowed up the car and headed for the stars overhead. Robert ran down the dirt road in hopeless pursuit for a few seconds, and watched intently as the craft disappeared into the night sky. Just like that his soul mate was gone. He stood alone in the darkness until the stars all faded from view with the coming sunrise.

# 22

## *Shock and despair*

Ross and Jessica sat at the edge of their chairs as their father finished the story. They had some questions, and he had answers for all of them. Robert told them, "I have never fully believed that my wife is dead, she has just been missing for all these years." Jessica was angry because she felt her father, and everyone else, had lied to her about her mother's death for all those years, but her father quickly cut her off by asking her, "Have you ever heard me refer to Janet as dead?" Ross chimed in "Dad always said that mom was taken away from us. Oh my God, that explains so much!" Both he and Jessica had always just assumed that was how their father classified death.

It certainly explained some things such as why they had never seen the car again, or their mother's body before the funeral. They had been told by the authorities that her body had been so badly burned in the accident that a farewell viewing wasn't possible, and come to think of it they were military representatives. As Ross spelled this all out verbally, he silently wished he had been privy to the information before encountering the alien species while exploring the Moon. He could have asked them if their previous scout missions had anything to do with his mother's abduction or not.

Ross paced back and forth across the room, and continued to connect the dots by realizing that the heavy burden of deep secrecy from 1947 and 1957 had taken an incredible toll on his father. It probably explained why the bottle became Robert's source of comfort more often throughout the years, and why he had never gotten truly close to Patty's mother Elizabeth. From Robert's point of view his wife Janet was still alive someplace, so he felt he would be unfaithful to her by taking another woman into his arms.

Returning to the reality of the present moment, Ross asked his father if anyone else knew of this shocking revelation. Robert shook his head sideways to signify the negative, but uttered that Grandpa Hank had taken the secret to the grave with him. The drugs to keep Robert awake were now losing the battle with the ever strengthening cancer inside of him, and he began to fade. Before falling asleep a few minutes later, Robert told his children that he knew it in his heart and soul that their mother was still alive somewhere. He didn't know how or when, but Ross and Jessica should never give up hope of her someday being returned to them.

Fighting through the tears of pain and confusion, Jessica looked at Ross for comfort and guidance. She asked him what he thought of their father's claims, and wondered if the medication had somehow created this delusion. Ross told her that he didn't think so, because Robert had clarity in his eyes that he had never seen before. He continued by saying "I visibly noticed how dad felt a sense of relief at finally being able to reveal what he had been keeping inside for so many years, and everything about all his claims made sense." She gave Ross a quizzical look after his final statement, so he checked to see if their father was indeed asleep before returning to his chair next to Jessica. He then leaned over towards the person he trusted more than anyone else in the world, and whispered into her ear "I have something incredible to tell you!"

# 23

*The bigger truth*

Having moved her to a position in the room that was as far away as possible from both the door and their father's bed, Ross once again leaned into his sister and began whispering into her ear. Before actually weaving the tale of the events that had taken place on the lunar surface, he demanded that Jessica keep the information she was about to hear in strict confidence. There was no way that he could risk anyone else, including his wife Patty, knowing what had happened to him and Dennis at this juncture, and he would need more time to evaluate whether he could ever release the information to the world. Jessica could tell by the look in her brother's eyes, and the added precaution of moving away from the door, that he was deadly serious about keeping the upcoming information a secret. Based on what she had witnessed about the news of Ross' presence on the base, she knew that secrets in this hospital did not exist.

Jessica listened intently to Ross as he whispered that he had encountered an alien life form while on the Moon, and she cupped a hand over her mouth in order to muffle her initial response. She composed herself before asking Ross to continue, but was still in awe of the information she was hearing. There was an alien species that had visited and charted over a thousand planetary systems throughout this part of the galaxy, and had been monitoring the development, or lack thereof, of life on this planet for more than two of our centuries. Ross occasionally needed to reach over to push her chin back up while he continued to tell the story. He couldn't really blame Jessica for having her mouth fall agape at the news, but once again demanded her secrecy.

Ross then informed her there was more to the story, as he pulled the necklace out from under his shirt collar. Asking Jessica if she remembered the item that once belonged to their grandpa; she nodded and whispered, "You received it from our father when grandpa died." A return nod from Ross preceded the next level of bombshell news, as he informed Jessica that the emblem belonged to the alien species they had been discussing, and he had found one just like it on the Moon.

For the first time that Ross could ever remember, his sister then made a ridiculously stupid statement by saying, "Are you trying to tell me that Grandpa Hank was actually an alien?" It was all he could do to keep from laughing out loud at the absurdity of her remark, but the expression on his face told Jessica all she needed to know. Ross calmly whispered, "You are far too intelligent to believe such a thing, and if you are going to be an idiot I will stop telling you the story right now!" Jessica knew her question had been ridiculous from the moment it came out of her mouth, but then again during this particular philosophical discussion about life altering events she wondered what, if anything, would be considered a stupid question?

She was then informed by Ross that their grandpa had received the emblem from his father when he was a young boy. Their great-grandfather had passed away long before either Ross or Jessica had been born, but the story was that he had retrieved the emblem from a crash site in 1897. He then gave it to his four year-old son as a present, and Grandpa Hank had held onto it for the next sixty-four years until passing it on to Ross. Grandpa had talked to Ross many times about the possibility of extra-terrestrial life when they would go fishing, and now Ross knew where his grandpa had formulated such an idea. Ross informed Jessica that their father would get mad at grandpa when he would discuss such matters with Ross, and that he definitely wasn't supposed to mention it around her. Jessica was only six when their grandpa had passed away, so it made sense to Ross why the discussions could never be had in her presence. She was just too young to understand, but now there might be added significance to keeping her in the dark.

With plenty of available time at his disposal, Ross had been thinking about their great-grandfather and grandpa at length on the way back from the Moon. His encounter with the aliens had helped him fit some pieces together, but what his father Robert had said recently added to the intrigue.

In a superior moment of clarity to counterbalance her earlier ridiculous notion, Jessica drew in a deep breath and now understood why Ross had said that their father's claims had made sense. The two of them had been able to read each other very well from the time they were kids in Rumley, and Ross instantly knew that Jessica was now also putting some things together. Ross said that he thought all of the events were somehow connected, but that didn't mean that their mother was still alive someplace else. He felt it would be ridiculous to entertain such a notion, and Jessica agreed. Ross did however know that it was an absolute fact that aliens were visiting and studying Earth, and it was also quite obvious that their father, grandfather, and perhaps even great-grandfather held a similar belief.

In what could not have been a more inappropriate moment, a knock on the door informed them that their father's current unstable life signs had triggered an alarm at the nurses' station, and he needed immediate attention.   Ross loudly agreed to allow the medical team to enter, and then whispered to Jessica that they should continue their discussion at a later time.

# 24

## *Robert's funeral*

The medical team at Fort Hood had done their best, but Robert didn't survive until Thanksgiving Day. Ross and Jessica had hoped that he wouldn't die on that specific day, and in that regard their wish was granted. During the late afternoon of Wednesday, Robert fell asleep for the final time. There had been a really close call the previous day when Ross and Jessica were having their private conversation in his room, but the Doctors had managed to keep him alive.

The next twenty-four hours had been difficult, as most of that time Robert was unconscious with extremely close monitoring. In the brief moments when he was awake, Ross or Jessica would tend to his needs while asking if there was anything else he wished to tell them. The questions themselves were unnecessary, but it seemed the appropriate thing to do. Both Ross and Jessica could tell by the look in their father's eyes that he had entered a quiet peacefulness by having said what he needed to say the previous day, and there was nothing more to add. Robert was tired of fighting the disease that now owned his body almost completely, and told his two children that he loved them both more than he had ever led them to believe. He smiled before closing his eyes, and soon after that the vital signs on the bedside monitor showed nothing but flat lines.

On the following Monday morning, a funeral service was held for Lieutenant Colonel Robert Martin on the base at Fort Hood, Texas. The event included all the pomp and circumstance associated with most military funerals, but wasn't attended by many people who were not stationed at the base. In truth Robert had more than earned both aspects of his final sendoff because he had served slightly more than thirty-one years in the Army before retiring in the winter of 1973, but had also become an abrupt and difficult man to get close to for more than the last quarter of a century.

After Robert had died, Ross put the wheels in motion with the appropriate personnel on the base for the upcoming service, and then needed to return to Houston for a few days of dealing with NASA and all the issues associated with the Moon mission. There would soon be a service for Dennis Strickland that the President, Secretary of the Navy, and other dignitaries would be attending, so Ross had to meet with his superiors to iron out some of the details and content of the impending eulogy. Jessica decided to take the road trip with her brother because there were a few things she needed to take care of back in Houston as well, and they would return to Rumley on Sunday evening. The time alone without interruption would also give the two of them a chance to further discuss the now increased alien influence upon the history of their family.

On Monday morning the entire family ventured over to Fort Hood for the funeral, and Ross became displeased that there were a few members of the media in attendance. As the honor guard moved Robert's coffin from the base chapel to the actual grave site, Ross had another flashback to the days of Grandpa Hank. He remembered the day of that funeral twenty-four years prior as if it were yesterday, and now he was seated between the same two people for another solemn event.

Now a man of thirty-five, he had a family of his own, and was very happy with all aspects of his life. He and his sister were both successful with their chosen path in life, his wife had given him the gift of two beautiful daughters, and he was one of only fourteen humans to set foot on the surface of the Moon.

Ross remembered when his father Robert had presented him with the flag from Grandpa Hank's coffin, and had requested that Ross perform a similar act with Robert's flag when the time came. Like it or not that time was now upon him, and he stood to salute the Army officer before accepting the flag presented to him on behalf of a grateful nation. His oldest daughter Aurora would need to remain strong for another moment or two, and that would be the most difficult aspect of the task. She was about three years younger than Ross had been when he received Grandpa Hank's flag, and she did not have the same closeness to her grandfather that Ross had enjoyed with his.

Ross stood in front of Aurora with the American flag tucked under his arm. In accordance with strictest military tradition the flag had been folded into a triangle shape with only the white stars on the blue background visible, and such a flag should always be treated with the upmost respect. Aurora liked the way her daddy looked in his dress white Navy uniform, with a few medals, ribbons, and the three gold stripes signifying his rank of Commander on each shoulder board. He had told her before that the gold pattern on the brim of his cap was another way of identifying his rank, but she could refer to them as scrambled eggs because that was what most other people called them.

He smiled and winked at Aurora as he motioned for her to stand up, while her grandmother Elizabeth prodded her with a little encouraging nudge. Earlier that morning Ross had showed Aurora how to salute before receiving the flag, and they had practiced just enough to make sure she had mastered it without the task becoming boring. She performed her duty perfectly without shedding a tear, which was more than could be said for her mother, grandmother, or aunt, and Ross leaned over to tell her what a great job she had done while also asking her to keep the flag safe. She verbally agreed to do so and placed the flag safely in her lap as she sat back down.

With that Ross let out a sigh of relief at knowing that the promise to his father of many years ago had been fulfilled, and he could now turn his attention to the upcoming funeral of his old friend Dennis.

# 25

## *Farewell to Dennis*

Less than three hours after the completion of his father's funeral, Ross caught a flight from Fort Hood to Cape Canaveral to attend the service for his fellow astronaut Dennis Strickland. It had already been a long and tiring day, but he had a few last minute details to go over with his superiors and the secret service for the event that was scheduled to take place the following morning. Tuesday would indeed be a busy day, as NASA would put on their best show in a salute to one of their fallen heroes for what would probably be a world audience, and then place the body on a plane bound for Colorado.

In spite of an offer by NASA and the Navy to bury Dennis at Arlington National Cemetery with a view of the National Mall, the Strickland family had decided to have Dennis rest within the family plot back in his home town of Woodland Park, Colorado. Many generations of their family had been buried there, and they wanted their brightest star to join them. The service was scheduled for Wednesday morning, and Ross felt sorrow for the Strickland family and the town who would most assuredly have their peace and quiet disrespected by the media.

It was a beautiful day along the Florida coastline as the large crowd of dignitaries gathered in honor of Navy Lieutenant Dennis Strickland, and the world media was predictably there in mass. Ross had a significantly larger role in these proceedings than those at his father's service the previous day, as he would be introducing and shaking the hands of some major power brokers. The crowd rose to its feet and applauded as Ross introduced the President of the United States, and then settled back into their seats for the ensuing speech. Ross followed that by introducing the Secretary of the Navy for a shorter speech, and then the senior NASA administrator so he could also have a turn. In each case the large bank of cameras hummed as he fired off a salute before receiving a firm handshake.

Ross concluded the speeches with a tribute of fond memories he and Dennis had enjoyed together from their early days at the Naval Academy, up through the events of the Moon mission. A twenty-one gun salute was followed by a formation of fighter planes that flew low overhead. As they passed overhead one of them peeled up and away from the formation to signify the loss of Dennis, and Ross once again snapped to attention. The American flag from the coffin was folded perfectly as in other military services, but this time Ross had to present it on behalf of a grateful nation to a grieving mother.

When Ross had first met Dennis during their Naval Academy days, he learned that his friend was born and raised in Colorado. As their friendship developed, it had been mentioned several times that Ross should someday visit Dennis' hometown at the base of the Rocky Mountains. Ross was saddened by the fact that through sixteen years of friendship with Dennis, and having met his parents on a few occasions, the timing had never seemed quite right for him to make that visit to Colorado. Now he was faced with visiting Woodland Park for the first time, and it was to bury his best friend.

As the plane transporting Dennis landed at Peterson Air Force Base in Colorado Springs, Ross caught his first glimpse of the surrounding landscape. He turned to Mr. & Mrs. Strickland on the opposite side of the aisle to see how they were doing, while offering an opinion of how beautiful the area was. It had indeed been a long day for the Strickland's, and the next day wouldn't be any easier. The motorcade moved through Colorado Springs and then northwest along Highway 24 to Woodland Park. With the aid of a police escort the distance was covered quickly, and something else about Dennis now became clear to Ross. He had inquired many years before why Dennis hadn't attended the Air Force Academy instead of Annapolis, but had been told it was because he wanted to spread his wings. Now that made perfect sense to Ross, as the town of Woodland Park couldn't have been much more than twenty miles away from the Air Force Academy grounds.

The following morning Ross sat next to the Strickland family just as he had done for the larger service back at Cape Canaveral. Along with a large group of family members, many friends and members of the local community had come to the service to pay their respects for Dennis, but the Governor of Colorado had been denied access. Ross understood their decision, and now their political influence. The Strickland family had been through enough of the pomp, and the Governor probably just wanted to get some free publicity.

The service was quiet, and Ross was impressed that the small contingent of media in attendance was fairly respectful. A few of them did manage to get close to Ross after the service for some questions about the Strickland family, but he handled the situation calmly by saying "They, and the nation, had lost a bright and dedicated talent at far too young of an age!"

# 26
## Holiday leave

On the evening of Wednesday December 4th, Ross returned to Houston and the much needed awaiting arms of Patty and the girls after what had been a circus of a week. Since his return to Earth nine days earlier, Ross had been in seemingly constant motion for the sake of three services that represented funerals for two people who had been a significant influence in his life. In terms of distance, the multiple flights and road trips paled in comparison to his recent journey to the Moon and back, but in many ways it had been much more exhausting.

During a significant portion of the aforementioned time, Ross had been in some sort of spotlight with the media for a variety of reasons. They had painted him as a hero of the first manned mission to the Moon in over a decade, the grieving son of a dying military father who had "somehow held on" until Ross' triumphant return, and then the grieving commanding officer and friend of a fallen astronaut. Ross couldn't believe how easily the world media had turned his life into a daytime television drama in such a short time.

NASA had been incredible in their support of Ross during the entire process, and had held off on some of the mission debriefing until the proverbial dust had settled. They did however want to speak with him at length the following morning, but promised him that after the full debriefing he could have thirty days leave. Ross knew he would be able to spend the Christmas and New Year's holidays with his family before returning to the office, but it would also give him time to keep his promise to Aurora. His now eight year-old daughter had been very patient with him since his return from the Moon, and she had shown her maturity when dealing with the wishes of her grandfather at the funeral. She and Ross had a handshake deal to go anywhere she wanted because he was on the Moon for her birthday, and Ross was fully committed to keeping that promise.

Just over a week later, Aurora got her birthday wish when she and her dad were joined by her mother and little sister for three days of fun at the beach on nearby Galveston Island. Ross wasn't really sure if it was a present for Aurora or for him, as three days alone with his family away from the still lingering media was fantastic. It was just what he needed to clear his mind from all the recent events, as the four of them had a wonderful long weekend on the beach. They built big sandcastles and splashed about in the water by day, and looked intently at the Moon while stargazing at night.

One night while the four of them sat on the beach together little Rachel sat in her daddy's lap and stared at his necklace. She pointed at the emblem and asked what the little markings on it meant, but Ross couldn't provide her with a good answer. All he could do was shrug his shoulders and tell his youngest daughter that he, or his Grandpa Hank, had kept the emblem for almost ninety years, but neither one of them could ever figure out what the strange markings on it meant.

Rachel continued her inquisitive path of questions by asking her daddy if he knew how many stars there were in the sky, so Ross put her down and turned himself around to face Patty and the girls. He scooped up a handful of sand and began to tell a story that had them all wide eyed with anticipation. He said to them that his handful of sand was like all the stars they could see in the sky at that moment, and then asked them all to look around at how much sand there was on the beach. When they finished and looked back at him in unison, he asked Rachel if she remembered the beach they all went to visit in Florida, and she nodded with a big smile. Then he told her that there were more stars than all the grains of sand on all the beaches around the world. Ross then had Rachel choose any one grain of sand from his hand that she wanted, and said that was like our sun that she saw during the daytime.

He concluded by saying that all the stars were not as close together as the sand in his hand, and she gasped in amazement at what her father had just said. Her older sister Aurora then looked at Ross and said, "That was way too many stars to ever count!", and Ross nodded in agreement as he stared deep into her eyes.

# 27

## Back to NASA

Ross had thoroughly enjoyed his thirty days of leave with his family, but it was time to get back to work. Jessica and Elizabeth had both joined the family for Christmas day, and the girls enjoyed seeing their aunt and grandma during a more festive event. Patty was glad to have everything seemingly back to normal, and felt good about the amount of rest that Ross had been able to get over the past few weeks. He had been reluctant to discuss the Moon mission, or Dennis, with her at great length, but she figured he just needed a little time to sort things out. Patty knew her husband well enough to know that he would eventually open up and talk to her about the accident, but didn't want to push him on the matter.

As Ross drove through the front gate at the Johnson Space Center, the guard asked if he could shake his hand. Ross agreed to do so while taking it as a complement, but hoped it wasn't a sign of things to come. Some would undoubtedly want to congratulate him for successfully landing on the Moon, while others would offer their hand in condolence for Dennis, but either way he could be in for a long day. He knew his co-workers meant well, but Ross didn't really want to shake hands with everyone that he ran into on his first day back at the office. There was after all a tremendous amount of work to be done by everyone, as the next scheduled space shuttle launch was now only a few weeks away.

He reported to the senior administrators just minutes after entering the building, and was informed of what was expected of him over the next several weeks. Ross would be tending to any questions the seven member crew of the upcoming orbital mission might have about launch and re-entry, while also taking part in the strategy associated with the follow-up missions to the Moon. His superiors had also determined that Ross should be one of the dignitaries in the crowd at Cape Canaveral for the upcoming launch, and he would therefore be spending a few days at the facility in Florida. Ross was still a well sought after figure in the eyes of the media, and NASA wanted to continue riding the wave of his popularity.

Once the crew of that launch was safely on its way, Ross would attend a press conference to discuss the importance of the current mission in the grand scheme of NASA's plans. After that he would return to Houston, and his work load would be centered on plans for the upcoming missions to the Moon and the subsequent construction of a long term habitat.

NASA had scheduled a launch date for a follow-up lunar mission aboard the Discovery in a few months, and Ross knew the short turnaround would keep the technicians and engineers responsible for getting her ready in time hard pressed. While specifics of the payload in the cargo bay had yet to be finalized, one important aspect of the mission had been predetermined. The plan was to have the Discovery land on or near the same spot that Ross had set her down, because that was where all the cargo and the rover vehicle was located. The two astronauts would then add their cargo to what had been intentionally left behind from the first mission, and power up the rover. At that point they would then locate and retrieve each of the three other rover vehicles that had been left on the surface by the final three Apollo missions. Each one of the old rovers would need to be fitted with a new power source that had been significantly improved since the time of their previous use several years before, and that would be a time consuming job. Due to the great distance that would need to be covered in order to complete the task, NASA had determined that the astronauts would be doing well if they could retrieve one rover per day.

Once all the rover vehicles had been collected, work could begin on a foundation for what would become a livable habitat for future astronauts. As Ross' knowledge of the lunar surface now exceeded that of anyone else ever associated with NASA, his input would be important in determining exactly how and where to begin the construction.

No further exploration of the far side would be scheduled for the second or third modern day missions to the Moon, because establishing the habitat was the top priority. The third mission of the Discovery, at a yet to be determined date, would carry a crew of seven whose only intended function was to use the rovers to assist in completing the structure from the mass of cargo that would be at their disposal.

# 28

## A morning of mourning

A large crowd of well-wishers braved the colder than normal temperatures associated with a space shuttle launch on a clear January morning at Cape Canaveral, and Ross was among them. Many of the spectators were cloaked in jackets, hats, scarfs, gloves, and whatever they could find to beat back the cold just so they could witness another launch of one of America's space shuttle fleet. After so many successes the act of a launch had almost become routine in many people's view, but it was still a fascinating spectacle to admire. In the midst of a thunderous roar signifying the engines springing to life, the space shuttle Challenger began to slowly move away from the launch platform.

With all eyes of the crowd pointed skyward while tracking the path of the rocket and the attached vehicle, Ross flashed back to the exhilaration of his three separate launches. They had all been very special moments in his life, but this was the same shuttle that had taken him as a rear seat payload specialist on his first ride into space. For that reason alone this specific shuttle, the Challenger, probably meant more to him than either the Atlantis, that he had piloted, or Discovery, when he had both commanded and piloted the mission. Ross didn't know yet if he would ever get a chance at a fourth ride on the most technologically advanced machine ever constructed by humans, but he sure wanted to.

Ross couldn't help but feel some level of envy towards the seven astronauts on the current mission as he watched the shuttle climb into the sky, and then it happened. Ross knew from the pattern of the trailing cloud of smoke that something wasn't quite right, but there was nothing that could be done. An instant later that unnatural pattern became even more pronounced as the main rocket and shuttle exploded into a huge fireball. For several seconds there was a collective mass of confusion within the spectating crowd, as no one knew exactly what was happening.

The explosion had occurred less than two minutes after liftoff, and trails of white smoke against the bright blue sky led away from the main circular cloud in three directions. Each of the twin rocket boosters flew randomly without any guidance, while the third source of smoke continued on the original flight path established before the explosion. That particular trail was created by what remained of the spacecraft as it lost its remaining momentum.

Within seconds the realization of the tragic event began to take hold within the thoughts of the crowd, and the screams of disbelief soon followed. Ross looked around to see that most of the spectators continued to gaze skyward, while some would ask a person standing next to them what had just happened before looking up once again. By then pieces of debris began to fall away from the distant white explosion cloud which made it resemble a fireworks burst on the 4th of July, but this was in no way a celebration of any kind.

Ross then heard some nearby people asking no one in particular if the astronauts could still be alive, but their question was greeted with silence. It soon became apparent that it was unlikely, but nobody wanted to verbalize the thought. Many of the huge camera arrays were still pointed skyward, and that could help NASA with the follow-up investigation, but some of the handheld cameras used by the news crews began to probe the crowd for suitable shots of grief. One such film clip would be that of family members who had just witnessed the death of a loved one, and how anybody could actually film that moment was beyond the comprehension of Ross.

The understandable level of confusion within the crowd continued in the following moments, but the NASA and law enforcement personnel acted quickly to reestablish a sense of order. They needed to clear the area of spectators as quickly as possible, but also needed to maintain a safe environment while doing so. Dignitaries such as family members of the astronauts and Ross were escorted to a safe haven away from the ghoulish members of the media, while others were directed towards awaiting vehicles. The members of the media however, were respectfully asked to stay in place until contacted by a NASA representative. Every frame of film footage that had been shot during the launch and short flight could be useful in helping to determine the cause of the catastrophe, so NASA wanted to take a look at all of it. As Ross took one last glance skyward at the explosive cloud that had just killed seven brave astronauts, he was struck with the harsh reality that he could have met with the same fate on any one of his three previous launches.

Understandably for many members of NASA, as well as the grieving family members and friends of the astronauts, the remainder of the day was somewhat of a blur. The first priority for Ross was to contact Patty to let her know he was safe, and that he would probably be detained for some time at the cape. She had not been watching the launch on television, and therefore was unaware of the tragic event until he informed her of it.  She broke into tears as he told her what had happened, and Ross knew she was reliving his previous launches with the same realization as his thoughts of a short time ago.

Next on the agenda was to meet with some of the senior NASA administrators, and discuss their next course of action.  By now everyone in the world with the means or desire to know about the tragic accident was becoming informed.  Film clips of the explosion had already been circulated by the news channels, and the major networks had cut into their regular programming with the breaking news.  Ross, like everyone else, was dealing with some level of shock and disbelief at what had just transpired, but he maintained his composure as best as he could before digging into what would undoubtedly be several months of investigation.

# 29

## The aftermath

In the days, weeks, and months that followed the Challenger disaster, the NASA investigation uncovered many flaws in the overall system. Without pointing fingers at specific individuals, a conclusion was reached that virtually all of NASA was to blame for the explosion of the space shuttle and the death of seven astronauts. Most everyone had assumed that the person next to them was so brilliant at their particular job that there was no need to double check their work. In short, NASA had become very complacent and self-convinced that their work was incapable of error. It was imperative that this mindset be changed before the space program could move forward again.

That level of self-enlightenment couldn't have come at a worse time for NASA, as that particular mission of the Challenger was directly on the heels of the Discovery mission that had cost Dennis Strickland his life. While facing a room full of hungry media, Ross and other representatives of NASA pointed out that the two costly missions had nothing in common. Ross and Dennis had been to the Moon on a very successful mission from a technical standpoint, while the Challenger had been destroyed due to technical malfunctions. The parameters of the two missions were vastly different, and everything needed to make a moon landing successful had gone off without any problems. Dennis had lost his life due to an accident in a very unforgiving place, but it had nothing to do with equipment failure. On the other hand, the seven astronauts onboard the Challenger had lost their lives in the blink of an eye on what was to be an orbital mission that was wrought with equipment failure.

The difference between the two was clearly visible to those who could think beyond the death tally, but unfortunately for NASA, most of the general public didn't see it that way. The ultimate truth was that a total of eight astronauts had lost their lives while on missions during a timeframe of less than three months, and a multi-billion dollar piece of equipment had been lost as well. In the midst of pressure from higher sources and the American public, NASA decided to postpone any future shuttle missions until all the apparent problems could be resolved. Their entire system of assembly and launch protocols would need to be revamped and tightly scrutinized, and it would probably be a few years until America launched another human being into space.

The ripple effect of that restructuring would prove even more costly to other aspects of NASA's plans, as the follow-up missions to the Moon for construction of a base were placed upon the scrap heap. Ross and Dennis had become the first humans to set foot upon the Moon in almost thirteen years, and it now suddenly appeared as if that gap in time could be repeated before any Americans would attempt a landing there.

There was one unexpected bright spot for Ross during the first few months after the Challenger disaster, and it was something that would allow him to bask in a little glory. He was notified by his former high school back in Rumley of an honor that would soon be bestowed upon him. The school board had decided to rename the baseball field after him in recognition of his accomplishments, and retire his former jersey number. He was after all the first person from Rumley to receive an appointment to one of the Military Academies, which was a notable achievement in itself. To then become an astronaut that had ventured to the Moon, put Ross over the top. The entire town, with one exception, was very proud of him, and turned out in full force at the dedication ceremony. After a brief acceptance speech from a place set up behind second base, a tarp was removed from the new structure next to the scoreboard. Now rising high above the outfield fence was a sign with the name, "Ross Martin Field" over the top of a huge number "51" near the area where he used to play left field.

Patty and the girls, along with Jessica, stood to applaud with the rest of the gathered crowd. Only the few people, who were standing close enough to Ross, near second base, could see him blush. At the diner back on Main Street, a tired and grumpy old man sat alone in silence with his cup of coffee instead of attending the ceremony. He had recently retired after many years of teaching at the local elementary school, but was never able to publicly admit that he had been so wrong about his former students' potential.

Later that day Ross and the family drove out to the old house that had been his childhood home. It had been a little over four months since Robert had died, and both Ross and Jessica had agreed it was time to sell the old place. They wanted to have one last look around before they put it on the market, and were surprised to see the old tire swing still hanging from the large oak tree in the front yard. Ross quickly decided he would take advantage of the opportunity to give both Aurora and Rachel a push for a few minutes, before Patty, and finally Jessica, each had a turn.

# 30

## A new frontier

Over the next several years NASA worked very hard to fix all that had gone wrong with their internal structure, and had eventually become ready for a return to space. There was a great deal of hype associated with the first scheduled flight, and the mission had been labeled and over sensationalized by the national media as the "triumphant return to space". Sadly, much to the dismay of NASA and the general public, that space shuttle mission would end up being postponed for a few months due to potential problems that were discovered within hours of the planned launch.

Ross had done his part during those difficult years for NASA as a trainer and consultant to the next generation of astronauts, and in the process had received another promotion to the rank of Captain in the Navy. Unfortunately with each passing year of the restructuring, and to some extent the over cautiousness of NASA to launch again, it had become clear to Ross that his days in space were probably over.

After much internal debate and soul searching, Ross decided in the summer of 1992 to try something new. Those close to Ross had given him sage advice about his chances of serving in public office, so he set his sights on challenging for a Texas House of Representatives seat in the upcoming November election. There were some local issues that both he and Patty felt strongly about, and they thought it could be a good way to help bring them into public view. The contingent of astronauts and their spouses helped Ross with some of the campaigning, while Patty worked on some of the mothers whose kids went to school with either Aurora or Rachel. Word of the well-liked and respected man's bid for the seat spread like wildfire, and the local area elected the native Texan to office.

The following morning Ross resigned his commission as a Captain and retired from the United States Navy with slightly over twenty years of service. It was now time to serve his country in a different capacity, as with the addition of his four years at the Naval Academy more than half of his forty-two years had been in the military.

Aurora, who would be fifteen in a few days, and Rachel, who had turned ten the previous June, stood proudly by their father's side with Patty during the farewell party at NASA. Jessica had been able to break away from her law office for the afternoon, so she was also there to wish her big brother well. The senior NASA administrator spoke in tribute to Ross for his seventeen years, as during that time he had been on three missions into space that included the last venture to the Moon. He had also helped train other astronauts for their respective missions, and had been a calming face for NASA when asked to step in front of the cameras and field questions from the media.

Ross worked hard at his new job within the Texas legislature, and made both friends and enemies because of it. He respected the views of his contemporaries, listened for information about any topic that could help him learn more about the new system he had entered into, and tried to do right by representing his district in a fair manner. In time he felt more comfortable with the job, and found a way to sway some former opponents over to his side on certain viewpoints. Ross introduced some legislation regarding benefits for veterans and people with physical disabilities into session, and then began to work on funding for educational goals within the state. At the completion of his two-year term, Ross was elected to a second term by a margin that exceeded his first. He continued to work hard, and was gaining support from those in his party.

In the meantime, his daughters were growing up fast. It had been decided by Ross and Patty when he was elected that the family would remain in Houston. That would ensure that the girls could continue to attend school with their friends, and Patty could stay close to many of the people she had met throughout Ross' NASA years. He would make the drive from Austin for the weekend whenever possible, and would be home during the times when the legislature wasn't in session.

During his second term in office Aurora had graduated high school, and then began her college years at the University of Texas in Austin. Ross thought her choice was perfect, because the campus is adjacent to the grounds of the Texas State Capitol Complex. It was easy for him to see her on occasion, and when Patty and Rachel came to town the four of them could have dinner together. When Aurora completed her first year of college in June of 1996, Rachel celebrated her fourteenth birthday. She had become a pretty young lady in her own right, and would be starting high school in the fall. Although Aurora had a few gentlemen callers, it seemed Rachel had all the boys looking in her direction. That would normally be an area of concern for any father, but Ross had faith that Patty and Jessica would monitor the situation.

# 31

## The logical step

Many of the same voices that had encouraged Ross to attempt local office were now in his ear again, and they spoke of loftier goals. He had done well during the previous four years for his district in the House of Representatives, and was getting to be well known throughout the entire Lone Star State. His political party had an aging member of the State Senate who was looking to retire, but wouldn't do so until the party found a respectable replacement. In the eyes of the party Ross was that man, so all they needed to do was to convince Ross of that fact.

The new job, if he was elected to it, would be relatively easy on the family. They could stay with the plan and remain in Houston, while Ross would only have to move his office from one side of the mammoth Capitol Complex to the other. He graciously accepted his party's offer, and put his name on the November 1996 ballot for Texas State Senator.

After the election had been won, the first thing Ross did was walk over to what would become his new office. He wanted to personally thank the man who he would be replacing for his endorsement, and asked if he could consult with him on a regular basis about the challenging topics that lay ahead. The loved and ageing Senator smiled broadly and clasped Ross' hand in a manner that reminded him of Grandpa Hank. He said it was evident that Ross was the right man for the job, and offered to help him with the transition in any way that he could. Ross took that opportunity to attempt to find out who in the Senate was a friend, and who was a foe. What could he hope to get accomplished as "the new kid" and what where some of the pitfalls he needed to avoid?

Throughout the next several weeks of instruction Ross acquired a new level of intelligence that was sure to help him with his new position, and was proudly sworn into office. Many of his personal items were transferred from the House wing to the Senate wing for him by his staff, but there were a few that he wanted to take care of himself. Several inquisitive looks were cast upon him as he made his way through the halls towards his new office carrying nothing more than a folded American flag in a triangular frame, and a brand new fishing pole with a red bow attached. Just as had been the case in his previous offices, Ross found a place in the corner for the fishing pole that was visible from his desk and put a nail in the wall nearby to hang the frame with the flag.

The next four years went by quickly, as Ross was working hard to justify his predecessors' belief in him. He had found it quite humorous during the previous winter when so many people had been caught up in the entire Y2K scare. In spite of all the unsubstantiated panic and speculation over the thought of all the computers crashing at the turn of the century, the world had survived. The entire thing seemed ridiculous when compared to some other events in the human endeavor, and Ross realized how easily the general public could be put into a panic by television or other aspects of the media.

By the time he celebrated his fiftieth birthday and began campaigning for a second term during the summer of 2000; Aurora had graduated from the University of Texas and was doing some accounting work at her Aunt Jessica's law office back in Houston. Rachel had just finished high school, and like most eighteen year-olds was ready to venture out and take on something new.  Patty had gone through a tough time earlier in the year, as her mother Elizabeth had passed away.  It had been a peaceful death, but with no siblings the brunt of the funeral logistics had fallen squarely on her shoulders.

The upside to the spring for Patty was when Rachel informed her where she had decided to attend college.  She would follow her mother's footsteps by attending the University of Maryland in College Park.  Patty was very proud of her, but warned Rachel against getting involved with a man from the nearby Naval Academy.  Her old friend and maid of honor Betty Collina was still living in the Washington D.C. area, so Patty knew that Rachel would have a local contact if she needed help with anything.

Ross won the election for a second term as Texas State Senator that fall, so he and Patty decided to accept Bettys offer to join her family for the Thanksgiving Holiday.  It would create a nice little break away from the rigors of Texas politics, and they would also have a chance to visit with Rachel who they hadn't seen since she started college a few months earlier. Patty and Betty had stayed in touch with each other over the years, and Betty had needed that friendship when she was going through the nasty divorce.  The personal visits between the two ladies had been too infrequent, but they hoped to get together more often now that the last of their respective children had grown up and headed off to college.  Ross hadn't seen Betty for several years due to scheduling conflicts such as orbiting the Earth in the space shuttle, or a legislative session in Austin, but she had called him with heartfelt condolences when Dennis had died.

During the entire Thanksgiving weekend it seemed like the three of them had never been apart. They picked up with conversations by the fire about all sorts of topics including the small informal wedding back in 1973 when none of them had any money to spare, and how life had run its course for each of them. They all raised a glass in a tribute to Dennis on the last night before Ross and Patty returned to Texas, and Betty shed a tear in thought of what might have been.

# 32

## *Reflection and change*

As wonderful as that Thanksgiving weekend had been, the following Thanksgiving would be different for the Martin family and all of America. Slightly more than two months earlier, the country had suffered a horrible attack upon not only its way of life, but on its own soil as well. The terrorist attacks of September 11, 2001 on New York City and Washington D.C. had given a complacent and blinded American public a taste of how far the human endeavor still needed to advance. Many civilians, and a few military personnel, had lost their lives in the attack, and the skyline of Manhattan had lost the iconic twin towers of the World Trade Center when they collapsed into a huge pile of rubble.

On the day after the attacks, Ross made sure that donations to the relief fund were made by all members of the Martin family. He also demanded that they all contact and maintain a correspondence with someone who had lost a family member during the horrible event. Meanwhile Ross, along with a few other State Senators, began spearheading a fundraising campaign within the halls of the State Capitol Complex in Austin that would enable several firefighters and medical personnel to travel to New York City so they could assist with the cleanup.

Ten weeks later Rachel came home from the University of Maryland to join the rest of the family in Houston for the Thanksgiving Holiday. She didn't want to come because she had an invitation to join her boyfriend's family in Philadelphia, but Ross and Patty were insistent that the family be together that particular year. Instead of the huge spread of food that had become the norm over the years, they all went to a homeless shelter to serve food and provide comfort to some of those less fortunate. There were no cameras or media at the shelter because Ross had informed no one other than his family members of their intent to help out. The visit wasn't done as a way to gain favor or momentum for an upcoming election like some politicians would have, but to remind his family members how fortunate they had all been for many years. It was a humbling experience for each one of them, including Ross, but they all felt better at the end of the day for having done so.

The next few years went by rather smoothly for Ross and the rest of the family, but the same could not be said for NASA as they had another huge setback. Although there had been multiple orbital shuttle missions with great success over the years, another accident had occurred that had claimed the lives of the entire crew.

On the morning of February 1, 2003 the space shuttle Columbia had broken apart, and burned up during re-entry into the Earth's atmosphere while over Texas. That event would once again put the American space program into a holding pattern until the problem could be identified and solved. Leading up to the time of the Columbia mishap, NASA had been increasing the duration of time in space for the missions, and that particular flight had been roughly the same duration as Ross' mission to the Moon. It was a sad day for all of NASA, and Ross, as he knew a few of the astronauts that had lost their lives. He had now been out of NASA for over ten years, but Ross still considered many of the people there friends, so he contacted a few of them to offer help and condolences.

A subsequent investigation had determined that a large piece of foam insulation had broken free from the external fuel tank, and had struck the leading edge on the left wing of the orbiter less than a minute after liftoff. The impact had damaged several of the heat tiles that protect the ship from the incredibly high temperatures associated with pushing through the atmosphere during re-entry, but it had gone undetected. The accident itself was bad enough, but for many there was added significance in the destruction because Columbia had been the first of the fleet to take flight. There was no way that the crew could have known the ship was damaged, or any way to repair it even if they had, so they paid the ultimate sacrifice like several others before them for mankind's quest of space.

Almost one year to the day after that sad event, while deep into his second four-year term as State Senator, Ross was once again approached by members of his political party to consider an opportunity. They had become disenchanted by the work, and political stance, of their United States Senator in Washington D.C., and informed Ross that his name had been put on a list of potential replacements. It was interesting to Ross how there had been a repeat of an earlier action, because he had served two terms of two-years each in the House of Representatives before being asked to step up into his current position. Now he was serving the second of two four-year terms in the State Senate, and had just been asked to step up once again.

This was the second time in his life that Ross had been put on a short list of candidates without knowing it, and it was sure to upset some people who thought their name should be on that list instead of his. Back at NASA, there had been a few disgruntled astronauts who thought Ross had moved through the rotation too quickly, and therefore should have never been given the Moon mission. In similar fashion, there were some politicians in Texas who would not be happy to hear that Ross had been presented with an offer to run for the coveted office of United States Senator.

His senior party members warned Ross that although they felt he could win the election, it would be much more difficult to unseat the current United States Senator from Texas. That man not only had a tremendous amount of support from the greater Dallas-Fort Worth area, but many of those in state and local offices were also considered his friends. Although flattered by the consideration of the party, Ross told them he would need some time to think about the offer and discuss it with his family before committing to the effort.

Later that afternoon he called Patty back in Houston to let her know he was coming home a day early for the weekend, and asked her if she could get Jessica and Aurora to come over one night for dinner. During the drive Ross had some time without any interruptions to reflect on the pros and cons of the offer presented to him, and one startling thought occurred to him. Ross would need to keep a watchful eye on that group of senior party officials who had presented him with the offer, because they might just want someone else to take over his spot sometime in the future. In fact, for all he knew they didn't really want him to win the United States Senate seat, but instead wanted to provide his vacated State Senate seat for someone else in the upcoming election. Ross had learned through some hard lessons during his time in Austin that politics can be a brutal business.

Soon after Ross arrived at the house in Houston, he and Patty began to discuss the possibility of his run for the office, and what it would entail. It was important to get input from the rest of the family, so Ross called Rachel in Maryland to ask her how she felt. That phone conversation, and the events of the following evening when Jessica and Aurora had come over, had provided Ross with the information he needed to make a rational decision. The entire family was in support of the idea, so on Monday morning back in Austin he informed the party members he would run at the next election.

Ross had roughly nine months to campaign before the election, and there were many things he would need help with. He and Patty contacted all their friends within the NASA family, while Aurora got in touch with many of her former classmates from the University of Texas in Austin. Jessica worked the angle of her contacts from her undergrad and law school days back at Rice University in Houston, and also asked her friends and colleagues in the law firm for help. The family also contacted disabled veterans, other people they knew in the military, the teachers unions, and anyone else who may have been aided by some of the earlier legislation that Ross had either introduced or supported. Once the word got out of his intent, he and Patty then hit the campaign trail to various areas of Texas to gain more support.

As the summer turned to the fall and Ross was gaining strength in the polls, his opposition began to get concerned. They started an advertising campaign to discredit Ross, but it actually turned in his favor. The opposition claimed that if Ross Martin was going to use his military service as a pilot and his days as an astronaut in conjunction with his time in state offices to solidify his credentials as a candidate for United States Senator, then it should also be pointed out that he had been shot down and had lost an astronaut while in command of a space flight. Their point was to imply that Ross must not have been very good at either job, or the results would have been better. He thought, as did many others, that it was dirty campaigning, and it was disrespectful to those who had lost their lives for America during dangerous and challenging situations. It was a political pitch in the dirt that the opposition was trying to get him to swing at, but his days of playing baseball in his youth, and at the Naval Academy, had taught him not to do so.

In spite of some people encouraging Ross to counter the attack, he just let it go. He expressed to those around him that he was treating it as "ball one", and he would be patient enough to let his opponent throw something he could swing at without damaging himself. Ross continued to learn what the citizens of Texas were concerned about as the campaign moved forward, and talked with as many of them as he could about how to improve those particular situations. In spite of having never campaigned near the Dallas or Fort Worth area because of his opponents close ties to the region, in November of 2004 Ross was elected by a narrow margin to a six-year term in the United States Senate.

# 33

## A seat on the Hill

A few days after most of the world celebrated the coming of 2005, Ross was sworn in as a freshman member of the United States Senate. He and Patty had spent the nearly two months since the election transitioning to the Washington D.C. area, which was rather hectic. The task was two fold in that they needed to find a new house, which Patty and her old friend Betty seemed to take charge of, and Ross needed to interview and hire his support staff.

Back in Austin his staff had done a nice job for him, but some of them were simply not yet ready for the national stage. The unfortunate aspect of that fact was that the one person he felt could make the transition had no intent of leaving Texas. She had been a wonderful assistant during both the House of Representative and State Senate years, but her husband, children, and newborn grandchildren lived in or a short distance from Austin, so she declined Ross' offer.

What Ross didn't know was that she had another reason for not following him to Washington D.C., but used the family scenario as a convenient excuse. Although he had always been a thoughtful and respectful boss towards her and the rest of the staff, she didn't agree with his viewpoints on certain subjects. With that in mind, she didn't feel that Ross belonged in a powerful position of national office, and therefore wouldn't assist him with the endeavor. Ross was understandably shocked at her stance, but respected her opinion and began a search for her replacement.

The first member to join his new staff was Jessica, who would be fifty years old in a few months. She was now a quite experienced lawyer in search of a new challenge, and this seemed like the perfect opportunity to push her personal envelope. It was a great fit, as Ross would need someone that he could trust who understood the law more than he did. His time in Austin had taught him much about the law, and how to create it, but Jessica had been formally educated in the field.

She also introduced him to Wendy Patterson, a rather short and plump spitfire of a woman from her law firm that she had known for several years. Mrs. Patterson had done a fantastic job at the firm, and for some of those years had served as the administrative assistant to the senior partner. Ross interviewed Mrs. Patterson a few times with Jessica, and they felt her intelligence, focus, and attention to detail could make her a valuable member of the staff if she was willing to brave the move to Washington D.C.

The senior partner was not at all happy with Ross for taking both women away from the firm, but as someone who had built the law office up from the ground, he could understand the ladies ambitions for larger opportunities. In time, Aurora would be leaving as well, but had agreed to stay on in her current accounting position through the coming April to help with the firm's taxes. That was not a problem for Ross as there was no immediate need for her in Washington, and by remaining in Houston for the additional time she would receive a valuable letter of recommendation for her dedication. She had turned twenty-seven shortly after the election, and both Ross and Patty were confident she would be able to continue her career when she made the transition to Washington D.C.

A bonus to the timing of the Martin family transition to the east coast was the ease of attending Rachel's December graduation from the University of Maryland. She had needed an extra semester to complete the necessary work for her degree, but the delay had meant the entire family would be able to attend the ceremony. Such a gathering would have been much more difficult during the previous spring, without taking valuable time away from the campaign trail back in Texas. Rachel was now twenty-two, had a long term boyfriend who would probably be her husband someday, and possessed no definitive career ambitions. Her only desire in life seemed to be that of becoming a mother someday.

Ross once again hung the triangular wooden frame that housed Grandpa Hank's flag on the wall near the corner, and placed the fishing pole next to it. He had now kept the two, with the help of both Jessica and Patty, in pristine condition for more than forty years. The fishing pole had still never been used, but Ross had occasionally changed out the red bow to keep it looking brand new. His new office area on Capitol Hill was larger than either one of the two he had occupied while in Austin, so he and his staff could comfortably settle in to begin a six-year term. They were all excited about their respective new jobs, and hopeful that they could make an impact on behalf of their home state of Texas.

# 34

## *The fishing trip*

When the United States Senate broke for summer recess during the first year of his term, Ross decided he needed a few days of alone time. Patty and her old friend Betty were planning on spending five days in New York City to see some Broadway shows and do some shopping, so Ross decided he would go on a little fishing trip. It had been years since he had been able to enjoy the peace and quiet associated with fishing, and this summer break from the office would give him the opportunity to do so. An old friend back in Austin had told him many times about a secluded spot in Texas where Ross could camp out in solitude and fish the nearby river, so the next day Ross caught a flight to Houston and a westbound connector to San Angelo. He rented a car, along with some camping and fishing gear for three nights of solitude, and a few hours later he set up camp next to the secret fishing spot along the Howard Draw well south of Ozona.

Early the next morning, Ross caught the first of what turned out to be several small trout, as the balance of the morning and afternoon fishing expeditions were quite productive. That evening Ross had just finished a fantastic dinner of trout cooked over the campfire when he heard a noise in the bushes. At first he thought it was a rabbit or other small creature, but he grabbed a solid piece of firewood to defend himself in the event it was a larger or more dangerous animal. Just then, an upright figure emerged from the bushes about fifty feet away from him. As it moved forward, Ross began to hear a voice in his head. The figure became clearer as it approached the campfire, and Ross put down the piece of firewood when he recognized it was the alien he had met some twenty years before on the surface of the Moon.

Ross wanted to ask the alien how he knew where to find him, but realized the question in itself would be ridiculous. An alien species as advanced as theirs probably had the ability to track the movements of anyone whenever they felt the need, and for some yet unknown reason they had decided to track Ross. He learned that the alien species wanted to minimize any further contamination of Earth, so this would be their only chance to discuss whatever was on Ross' mind. Throughout their most recent observational rotation of this and the neighboring three solar systems, the alien had become a pest towards his superiors while attempting to convince them that further communication with the astronaut from ₹-829-ʒπ-3 was necessary. He had reluctantly been granted this one and only visit due to his persistence, but it had been permitted largely in part because of the way Ross had behaved towards the two aliens while on the surface of the Moon. The alien species also felt it was a perfect opportunity to learn more things about the human species from Ross.

With that Ross reached out to shake the hand of the alien, before motioning for him to have a seat on the large log next to the campfire. Ross began by asking about the emblem on the necklace that he still wore as he pulled it out from underneath his shirt collar, and was relieved to learn that there was truth to the story his Grandpa Hank had always told him. The alien confirmed that a scout ship had crashed due to mechanical failure during what Ross' people identified as 1897 in western Texas, and that it had been part of a formation of nine ships. Grandpa Hank's father must have removed the emblem from the uniform of a dead pilot, before they buried the bodies. It had been quite lucky for the aliens that the contamination of the planet had been so minimal in that instance, because mass communication technology of the inhabitants was in its infancy and they had also not yet mastered the ability to fly.

Ross told the alien that if his great-grandfather, and the other men who witnessed the event, had reported seeing a flying machine crash to the ground they would have been thought to be crazy. Ross then asked the alien if he knew the pilots who had died in that crash and the alien responded that he had known one of them very well.

Suddenly remembering what his daughter Rachel had asked him many years before, Ross inquired about the meaning of the tiny little etchings on part of the emblem. He continued by saying that neither he nor his grandfather could ever make sense of it. Ross informed the alien that there were many different forms of written language on Earth, but only the first of the six symbols resembled anything they he had ever seen before. It looked very similar to a lower case "I" in the language that their family used.

Continuing his line of questions, Ross asked if they usually flew their scout ships in a formation of nine, and had any other crashes ever occurred? The answer to both questions was yes, so the alien offered an explanation. He reminded Ross that the aliens had been observing the planet from their small base on the Moon for more than two centuries of Earth time, and had made multiple scouting flights close to the planet

152

surface during that time. He also informed Ross that his ancestors had visited and observed the planet for research several times in the more distant past, and had left markings and temples at various locations around the planet that were still considered a mystery by most of the inhabitants of Ross' world.

To the question of crashes, there had only been one other on this continent since the time of the crash of 1897. Ross learned that it was one of the nine scout ships under the command of the alien who was telling him the story, as he had been the flight leader of a formation that was getting a closer look at certain areas of ₹-829-ঽυπ-3. Because several atomic signatures had been recently detected on this continent, along with a few actual detonations both here and on a smaller land mass on the opposite side of the planet, the aliens had decided to investigate. While listening to the specifics of the flight path, Ross concluded that they had flown over an area of Tennessee that had been used for the early experimental research of the atomic bomb, and then Washington where a different aspect of the Manhattan Project had been developed.

The alien continued by saying that the formation of nine ships had been spotted and reported by a human in a flying machine near the tall mountains of what Ross figured to be the Cascade Range in Washington State, but had not taken evasive action. The mission continued towards the area where the first atomic detonation signature on this continent had been registered, and that was when the other crash had occurred.

The official alien recollection of the event was that an atmospheric disturbance had struck one of the scout ships and had caused it to crash near where the first modern era atomic detonation had taken place. It suddenly occurred to Ross that the alien was discussing the New Mexico crash of 1947 outside of Roswell, and what a weird coincidence that was for the Martin family.

Unfortunately for the alien species, their plan of limited contamination of the planet would take a serious setback because of that crash. Due to the technological advancements, and increased communication abilities, of the inhabitants of the planet during that fifty Earth year span, it was much more difficult to keep the crash of a supposed alien spacecraft a secret. Ross knew all too well about the crash and subsequent investigation that surrounded the Roswell event they were speaking of, because his parents Robert and Janet had met while being part of the investigative team.

It was obvious that the alien knew the pilots who had died in that crash because they were under his command, but he didn't seem to be as moved by their death as he had been when discussing the deaths of the earlier crash. Ross wondered if his great-grandfather may have taken the emblem from the uniform of an alien who meant as much to this alien as Dennis had meant to Ross.

When the question of each other's physiology became part of the discussion, Ross couldn't help but look at the feet of the alien. As had been the case on the Moon, there was no part of the aliens clothing that covered that area of their anatomy. Ross thought they looked to be very thick skinned and must be incredibly durable to never need any type of covering. There were three long skinny appendages that were similar in appearance to the fingers on their hands, but they were set into a tripod formation and strong enough to raise and lower the body like when a human stands on only the toes. Ross could see no fourth appendage like on the hand, but because the aliens thumb was so high up on the wrist it was possible their foot had something similar that was hidden by the uniform. The strength of their feet and the grip of the handshake had proven to Ross that even though the alien body looked to be frail, it was far from it. With the glove of his spacesuit on, Ross couldn't feel the pressure of the handshake some twenty years before on the Moon, but his hand was still a bit tender from the greeting of this encounter.

The aliens head was hairless and slightly larger to the scale of their body as opposed to humans, with distinguishing characteristics such as eyes and small ears. There was nothing below the large black eyes that could be interpreted as a nose, and the mouth served only as a way of taking in sustenance as opposed to communication.

Ross also finally noticed that the alien was not wearing a breathing apparatus like he had on the Moon. He concluded that the atmosphere on their home world must be similar to that of Earth, because there was no current sign of labored breathing by the alien. The atmospheric pressure, or lack of it such as on the Moon, apparently had no effect on the skeletal structure of the alien species, but they did need some sort of atmosphere to breathe.

The clothing the alien was loose fitting, but was gathered tightly at the neck, wrists, and ankles, so Ross asked about that. He learned that the clothing was used more as a filter to help protect their major organs and gills from dust and other pollutants that could be encountered on worlds other than their own, because they were quite sensitive.

Space flight and timeline differential were the next topics on Ross' mind, so he listened intently as the alien projected his thoughts on the matter. Their species had long ago developed a way to travel through space much faster than the speed of light, which was far beyond the current capabilities of the human space endeavor. The life expectancy, and the way the alien species calculated time, was also much different than that of the dominant species of ₹-829-૩π-3, or Earth. That was why the most recent observational rotation by the alien through the neighboring systems of less than a month in his time was equal to twenty years of Ross' time on Earth.

While listening to the explanation of all this, Ross asked how Earth came to be known as ₹-829-૩π-3. The alien used his long index finger to scratch the symbols into the dirt so Ross could see them, and then informed him that the first symbol of ₹ signified the quadrant of the galaxy that this solar system resided in. The 829 was simply the number of the slightly over one-thousand that had been explored in the quadrant. He continued by informing Ross that the ૩π-3 was there to identify that both language and math skills existed on the third planet from the host star. ૩ was the symbol used for language, while π represented math.

Ross informed his alien friend that humans also used π as one of their most significant math symbols throughout the world, and the alien informed him that was probably due to his own ancestors influence during long ago observations of this planet. Ross had also seen the symbol ૩ someplace before, but couldn't place exactly where. He seemed to remember that it was from some ancient language here on Earth, but his knowledge of those early texts was quite limited. It became obvious to Ross that the current system of numbers widely used on Earth was indeed universal, and was also a derivative of earlier alien influence, while the much lessor used Roman numeral system probably wasn't.

At the conclusion of their educational exchange of information, Ross stood to offer thanks and his hand in friendship. The alien shook Ross' hand with his three fingers reaching clear up to his wrist before slowly pointing towards the necklace with his other hand. He informed Ross that it was a nice tribute to the alien species that he continued to wear the emblem around his neck, but it was upside down. The alien claimed that the facsimile had been orientated and displayed correctly on the Moon vehicle, and Ross realized that was because it was floating upside down as opposed to the way it had been placed on the chain. All these years he had thought that the only loop in the symbol belonged at the top, but apparently he was wrong. There was no way that Grandpa Hank could have known any better, as he had simply run a chain through the only loop of the emblem so it could be worn as a necklace. Faced with that same level of ignorance, Ross had just accepted it at face value.

# 35

## A new generation

Slightly over eleven years later, in November of 2016, Ross' family and staff were celebrating many things including another election victory. Ross was happy that the citizens of Texas had already seen their way clear to provide him with two six-year terms in federal office, but he knew there were many more things he wanted to accomplish.

During the two terms Ross had become involved with several pieces of legislation that had become law, served on a few committees, and had made many friends, but there would always be something more that could be done. It had been a long and grueling campaign, perhaps the roughest of all that he and the family had been through, but it was worth it. In spite of the challenges that lay ahead, now was the time to exhale, even if only for one night.

Another cause for celebration was the birth of their second grandchild Janet, who had come into the world just three days before the election. Ross had turned sixty-six the previous summer, Patty would soon be sixty-five, and their youngest daughter Rachel, who was now thirty-four, had provided them with two beautiful grandchildren. She had married her college boyfriend ten years earlier, and had worked for roughly five years in the private sector before giving birth to a son named Luke in the summer of 2012. Luke's and Ross' respective birthdays were one week apart, and the two of them had enjoyed blowing out the birthday candles on their cake together during the most recent celebration.

The newest addition to the family was named after the grandmother that Rachel never knew, and that made Ross and her Aunt Jessica very happy. They were both confident that little baby Janet would carry on their mothers' name proudly, while Patty just loved the fact that there was now another healthy grandchild to spoil.

The final reason for the festive mood within the Martin family was the one that took place every year at this time, as Aurora would celebrate turning thirty-nine in a few days. She had decided many years before that her career was more important to her than raising a family of her own, but loved the fact that she was now an aunt for the second time. Things could not have been better for Ross and all those around him, but there was little doubt that the coming year would hold tremendous challenges for him and the family.

Slightly over two months later, Ross tilted his head back as far as it would go and gazed at the magnificent mural painted on the ceiling of the United States Capitol rotunda. The mural depicted some history of the United States, which he was pleased to point out to his grandson Luke as they looked at the pictures. A moment later Rachel came over and smiled at them both before she retrieved Luke away from her father. Then they, along with the rest of the family, moved towards their seats. Patty stepped up and gave Ross a hug and a peck on the cheek, then used her thumb to remove the trace of her lipstick she had left behind before faking an adjustment of his already perfect tie. She said, "You deserve this", as she moved towards the door and took the arm of her military escort for the short walk to her seat next to their daughters. She then sat patiently along with everyone else.

Ross wondered how many of the men who had come before him had actually aspired to this moment, as he certainly had not. When he was a boy in Rumley he wanted to be a professional baseball player, but that had not panned out. A few years later he set his sights on becoming an astronaut, and that dream had come to fruition. He had worked hard his entire life and felt he had done a good job serving his country in many different roles, but he had never dreamed until recently that this day would come.

On this clear and crisp January day of 2017, he was about to be sworn in as the 45th President of the United States, and he still didn't quite understand how he got there. Ross had been married to Patty for almost forty-four years, but they had never spoken once about someday residing in the White House as the Chief Executive and First Lady until less than two years prior to this moment. They, like all married couples, had seen the good times and the bad, but found a way to make it work. Throughout the early military deployments, the dangerous yet exhilarating space shuttle flights during his NASA years, the extended time away from home while serving in state or federal office, Patty had faithfully stood by him. She had given him two beautiful, intelligent, and successful daughters, so she deserved to be called the "First Lady" in his eyes.

His sister Jessica had also been an instrumental part of his overall success. She had been his partner since the earliest days of their childhood, been a close friend to Patty during the lonely times, and a wonderful aunt to the girls throughout their entire lives, but it went beyond all that. Jessica alone held the ultimate secret that Ross had kept from the public and his wife and children throughout the years, so he knew deep down that she was the one he trusted most. On top of that, her legal skills had proved to be most valuable to Ross during his two terms as United States Senator, so he was the one who felt privileged when she had agreed to become part of his White House staff for as long as he occupied the office.

Ross smiled broadly as he realized he could finally give his kid sister, who still wore the leg brace, a birthday present worthy of how much she meant to him. Jessica would be able to celebrate her sixty-second birthday in grand style, as she would join the first family at several inauguration balls later that evening.

His moment of peaceful contemplation was then interrupted by the secret service agent on his personal detail who informed him that it was now time to go. With a nod of acknowledgement, and a handshake of thanks for what the man was sworn to provide, Ross moved towards the door for the short descent of stairs to the podium.

For as far as the eye could see along the length of the National Mall spectators stood and waited for their newly elected President to emerge from the Capitol, and then showed their support via thunderous applause when he came into view. Ross knew some of them had not actually voted for him, but they had come to see a moment in history and for that he was thankful.

He shook the hands of several people as he made his way to the podium where he would take the oath of office, and gave a broad smile to the four most important women in his life, his lone son in law, and his two grandchildren before taking his position. Luke, now four and a half, was old enough that he would remember the events of this day, but Janet would have to be informed later that she had witnessed a presidential inauguration from no more than twenty feet away when she was less than three months old.

Ross put his left hand on the bible, raised his right hand, and took the oath of office. In the blink of an eye it was over, and the nearby Marine Corps Marching Band played "Hail to the Chief" as he was now officially the President of the United States. After congratulatory handshakes from the Supreme Court Chief Justice, outgoing President Barrack Obama, and a kiss from Patty, Ross delivered his acceptance speech. A throng of people, perhaps more than one-hundred thousand strong, had braved the long wait in the cold to witness the event, and a television audience of millions throughout America and other parts of the world had joined them.

A short time later Ross clasped the hand of Patty, and climbed the stairs back into the warm confines of the Capitol Building with their daughters and the rest of the family following close behind. Once back in the rotunda there was a group hug, which was then followed by seemingly endless handshakes with members of Congress and other well-wishers. President Ross Martin and Patty were then escorted by the secret service to the waiting Presidential motorcade for the long slow drive towards the White House, as a multitude of jubilant observers cheered them on.

# 36

## 1600 Pennsylvania Avenue

Although Ross knew there would always be something to attend to while he held the office of President of the United States, he decided that he owed it to himself, and the rest of his family, to exhale for the remainder of his first day in office. The upcoming multitude of formal inauguration balls that evening would surely lead to the first of what would be many nights of less than adequate sleep during the next four years, so he wanted to relax beforehand. He would become fully immersed in his new responsibilities the following day, but he wanted to explore every inch of the White House with Patty. That would give them both an opportunity to meet with each member of the staff, so they could personally thank them in advance for their hard work and dedication. Ross also planned to make a few phone calls from his new desk in the oval office when their exploration was completed, because there were several people from around the country who he intended to invite to the White House in thanks for helping him win a very close election.

His old friend and Annapolis roommate Shaun Jamison had become a prominent businessman in the Boston area, and had throughout the years become a strong advocate of rights for people with physical disabilities. Shaun had been working closely with Jessica to help gather financial support and votes for Ross from disabled veterans and others who faced daily challenges due to physical limitations. When they spoke of Ross' historical voting record at both the state and national level in support of rights for the disabled, the word spread quickly around the nation. Their combined efforts helped Ross to overwhelmingly carry a previously uncalculated demographic of American society, and in some cases was the difference in winning a county or state.

Another Annapolis roommate, James Franklin, had done his part by helping with some much needed support in the Pacific Northwest. After retiring from a lengthy stint in the Marine Corps, James returned to his hometown of Seattle and started up a private security business. He and his personally trained staff had been responsible for providing protection for a few local politicians or wealthy businessmen over the years, and James used those connections to their fullest by requesting that some of those people endorse Ross for President.

Ross also received help from members of Dennis Strickland's family in Colorado. Although Dennis' parents had both passed away many years before, the family had always been aware of how close Dennis and Ross had been. It was their pleasure to use the family name and local political influence to help Ross with the election, so he had won the Electoral College votes of Colorado with ease.

Another demographic that sided with Ross was that of the military. He was rightfully thought of as "one of their own" because he had served in active duty for nearly a quarter of a century, and earned additional respect by seeing front line action in a foreign war. In that regard it was much easier for an active member of the military to address him as Commander and Chief as opposed to someone who had never worn a uniform.

The only contact from his days at the Naval Academy that Ross didn't seek help from during the campaign was the last of his original roommates. Davis Lee Wakefield III had been an almost constant source of anguish during their time together at Annapolis, and had by last reports fallen on bad times. He had somehow found a way to squander the fortune that had been left to him by his parents, and in turn their family name carried little, if any, weight in South Carolina anymore.

In spite of the turbulent history that existed between the two men, Ross gave Davis Lee a call several months before to see if he needed anything. They were after all brothers of the Naval Academy class of 1972, so Ross wanted to make sure he was doing all right. Davis Lee carried sharpness in his tone when he said "I can't believe a man who decided years ago to side with our two Yankee roommates, instead of a southern brother, is attempting to become the next President of the United States. There is no way that I need, or will accept, any help from such a traitor!" At that moment Ross knew that they would never have any further contact, and if he was to win the election he would inform the Secret Service to keep a watchful eye on the future actions of Davis Lee.

Now at his desk in the oval office Ross had completed the calls to the list of those he wished to thank, and was about to venture upstairs to the residence when Mrs. Patterson knocked on the door. Wendy had been his personal assistant for the twelve years he had served in the United States Senate, and there had never been a doubt in Ross' mind that she would continue her excellence as a member of his White House staff.

As had always been her custom, she moved through the door without waiting for Ross to reply and offered an apology for the interruption. She informed Ross that she had just received a call from the Commandant of the Naval Academy, and he was respectfully requesting a moment of the Presidents time. With that Ross picked up the phone and greeted the Admiral on the other end of the line. A moment later Ross said he would be honored to do so, and would make sure his schedule remained clear.

As he hung up the phone and vocally summoned Mrs. Patterson back into the office, he glanced over to where the fishing pole and Grandpa Hank's flag had their place of honor. Ross had placed them next to the mantle of the fireplace, which was the only spot in a room absent of corners that the fishing pole could lean without potentially falling over. He then took a glance and reached out to rub the emblem that he had worn around his neck for so many years. Before beginning his recent phone calls, Ross had removed the necklace and hung it from the reading lamp on the Presidential desk as a constant humbling reminder of his limited power.

As Wendy entered the oval office Ross beamed with excitement, and announced to her that he had just accepted an invitation to give the commencement address at the Naval Academy graduation for the class of 2017 during the upcoming spring. He was as honored to celebrate his forty-five year anniversary of graduating from the academy by delivering the speech, as they were to have him do so. Annapolis had just equaled the United States Military Academy at West Point by having a second graduate become Commander and Chief, and wanted to honor President Ross Martin for doing so.

# 37

## The twilight term

The election of 2020 had gone much easier than the previous one, and President Ross Martin won a second term in office by an overwhelming margin of nearly seven to three in the nation's popular vote. Within the Electoral College the margin had been even more lopsided, so Ross, and the remainder of his political party, had much to smile about.

The first four years of his presidency had gone very well for Ross and the nation as a whole, so the citizens of America had shown their faith in his ability to run the country for an additional four years. Of course those first four years almost didn't happen, as Ross had won the election of 2016 by the narrowest of margins in a clean campaign that had a competent and viable candidate representing both sides of the isle. That in itself was somewhat of a shock for the standards of any election, but Ross had emerged as the man to follow the eight years of Barrack Obama. In this particular election, the other major party had put up a candidate that most viewed as inferior to Ross. That coupled with the positive upturn in the economy during the previous four years, had made the choice obvious for many of the voters.

Ross had become a seventy year-old man while on the campaign trail the previous summer, but looked and felt much younger. He had taken care of himself physically since he was a boy in Texas, and that attention to his health was paying off a dividend during his so called senior years. Patty was also still in good health, but her long straight blond hair of yesteryear had been replaced by a shorter cut of grey.  She still possessed the intoxicating eyes and beautiful smile that had caught the attention of Ross nearly sixty years before, and he still believed a room looked better when she was in it.

Roughly four months after the election, a lull in the schedule would allow Ross to have a little downtime.  In typical fashion the holiday season had been rather hectic, and that had been followed by his fifth state of the union address to Congress and the American people.  February had then brought forth lots of foreign travel for diplomatic reasons, so Ross was ready to take advantage of the opportunity for a few days of peace and quiet.  Normally in early March he would venture back to Texas if the schedule permitted, but in this case he felt the need to do something different.

The winter along the eastern seaboard had been rather mild that particular year, so there wasn't much snow to speak of.  With that in mind, Ross decided to visit Camp David in northern Maryland with as minimal amount of staff and secret service as possible.  Ross really enjoyed the retreat that had been used by every President on numerous occasions during all seasons for well over half a century, but he usually only went there in the summer months.  No one else in the family had ever really liked the retreat very much, especially in the winter time, so Ross knew he wouldn't hurt anybody's feelings by not inviting them.

With the exception of the White House itself, the grounds of Camp David were perhaps the most secure location on the entire planet for the President of the United States.  For that reason it became a favorite place for Ross to visit as often as possible.  Only there could he take a long walk through the woods by himself with no secret service standing in his shadow, so it was a great place to think. His protection detail knew to give him plenty of space, but Ross had agreed to always carry a whistle in the event he needed their assistance.

On this particular solitary walk, it also became a place where he was visited by an old acquaintance. As Ross rounded a gentle corner of the walking trail through the woods, a familiar figure was standing some twenty meters in front of him. He smiled, looked around carefully in all directions before speaking, and then softly said, "Hello old friend. It's good to see you, but why have you returned for another visit?"

Ross had not expected to ever see the alien again, because their last meeting of nearly sixteen years before was supposed to be a final contact. At that time Ross had been informed that the aliens wanted to avoid further technological or spiritual contamination of Earth, so Ross was understandably surprised as he reached out with a welcome handshake.

Ross believed that the main topic of their conversation would be the human space endeavor, or recent lack of it, because mankind had not returned to the Moon since his mission more than thirty-five years before. Even the shuttle program had been discontinued for nearly a decade, as Atlantis had flown the final mission in the summer of 2011. The fleet had frankly outlived their original intended life span, but at this time there was no replacement that could serve as the next generation vehicle. All was not lost however, as in spite of drastic budget cuts to NASA during the time of Barrack Obama's administration, the space program had not been completely abandoned. There was still an ongoing American presence at the International Space Station, but those astronauts needed to hitch a ride with the Soviets in order to get there. NASA was also involved in a few other unmanned projects, and had been able to get some good results with a program that sent small robotic probes to the surface of Mars.

The budget cuts to NASA had been necessary to help rebuild a national economy that had been left in ruins by former President George Bush, and Ross knew all too well that many other segments of American free enterprise had been hit just as hard. It had been a long slow process to bring back a healthy and robust economy for the nation, which had literally taken the entire eight years of the Obama administration and the first three of Ross Martin's. With the unemployment levels back down to more satisfying numbers, and a strong housing market in place, Ross felt he could use his second term in office to help reestablish a larger budget for NASA. If successful, perhaps mankind could soon return to the Moon to construct a long term livable habitat as had been planned in the 1980's.

As had been the case during their two previous encounters, Ross could hear the thoughts of the alien without ever seeing his mouth move. Unfortunately for Ross, his jaw fell wide open soon after they began to communicate. The alien had not returned to discuss how the people of ₹-829-ॐπ-3, or Earth, had been advancing with their space station or the new wave of robotic probes sent to explore Mars, because they were well aware of that activity from their observations of us. The alien wanted to discuss something entirely different, but it did involve space.

Ross listened intently as the alien projected his thoughts towards him, and learned that the people on Earth who are responsible for gaining knowledge by studying the stars would soon discover that a large asteroid is headed in this direction. The discovery of the object will intrigue them enough to take a closer look at the trajectory, but they will inherently want to disbelieve their findings. Further meticulous examination will reveal that an impact is eminent, and they will not know what to do about it.

The alien continued by revealing that he had been sent to Earth by his superiors to inform Ross that the impact of that asteroid will alter the conditions that support life on the planet significantly. Although some may survive, most of the inhabitants be they human, animal, or plant life will perish. In conclusion, Ross heard that this knowledge was given to him well in advance of any discovery by the scientists of this planet. The reason for that was because of what Ross had done to help the alien tend to his friend during their first contact while on the surface of Earth's moon. His humanitarian actions then, and at other times during his life, along with those of some other people from various areas around the planet, had showed the aliens that the human species had potential beyond the technological side. Their continued observations had also indicated that Ross currently held one of the most prestigious and powerful positions on the planet, and was therefore in a position to help save some of the species.

The news was beyond shocking, but Ross also knew that the source of the terrible information was reliable beyond the comprehension of most people on Earth. He knew he had to speak with his top scientific advisors as soon as possible about what was going to happen, and then somehow explain how he knew it was going to take place. Ross asked his alien friend the two part question of how long it would be until the astronomers of Earth discovered the asteroid, and how much longer after that would it be until the actual impact? What he heard as the response to his questions made Ross feel sick to his stomach, as he was informed that in roughly half a cycle around our host star the discovery would be made, and after that it would be almost one additional cycle before the impact. The main reason for the delay in the discovery was because Earth currently was in a position on the opposite side of our host star from the incoming direction of the asteroid.

Ross' head was spinning at the thought of all that had been presented to him in the last few minutes, and his first action at the conclusion of this encounter would be to speak with his sister Jessica about it. He quietly thanked his alien friend for the incredible, yet horrifying, information and his civilizations' concern about the people of Earth. Ross offered a quick handshake, and took a look around in all directions before they went their separate ways.

It appeared they had not been seen or heard by any of the secret service who would be patrolling the woods, but only time would tell. After roughly a dozen steps Ross glanced back over his shoulder to see if he could still see the alien, but he was nowhere in sight. He suddenly remembered that the alien species had become quite adept at visiting and studying Earth without being detected, except on those rare occasions when they either wanted to be seen, or one of their scout ships had crashed.

Ross quickened his pace as he walked back towards the cabin, and waved his whistle in the direction of the nearest secret service agent as he emerged from the woods. There was much discussion and work to be done within the allotted time frame specified by the aliens in order to save lives, so he best get to it.

Back in his cabin, Ross pondered briefly over his next move before giving the order for Jessica to be immediately flown over via helicopter from the White House. He intended to speak with no one else before her arrival, and informed his guard outside the door to make sure he wasn't disturbed until she arrived.

A few hours later when Jessica knocked on the door, Ross invited her in and said that he hoped she had brought some good walking shoes. She nodded positively sensing that her brother was concerned about something, and then said "I'm getting plenty of exercise, and I'm not currently having any trouble with the leg." Ross responded with "Glad to hear that, but the upcoming walk is not just for exercise sake because I have something very important to discuss with you!" With that she put down her briefcase, and walked over to him to ask what was bothering him. He asked Jessica to follow him out onto the walking trail so they could talk, and then he waved the whistle towards the nearest secret service agent as they reached the edge of the woods.

A few minutes later Ross stopped at the same spot where he had communicated with the alien, took a good look around in all directions to ensure their privacy, and then leaned towards his sister to whisper the latest revelation into her ear. Jessica listened intently for a few minutes until Ross backed away, and then took a step back herself in shock and disbelief. She tried her best to remain composed, but she began to tremble and then became wobbly enough that Ross had to grab her arm to keep her from falling down.

When the initial shock began to wear off Jessica asked Ross if he was sure about what he had told her, but he could only shrug. Ross said "I don't have the proof yet, but why would the alien species fabricate something as hugely significant as the potential extinction of the human race?" He continued by saying that "The aliens obviously have the advanced technology to be able to track such events within the cosmos, and land here undetected if they wish." Jessica steadied herself as she listened to what her brother had to say, but was still fighting the powerful emotion of denial. Ross then added to his previous comments by informing her that when he first encountered the alien on the Moon he was told they would return at regular intervals to their base on the far side for continued observations of our planet.

Jessica asked her brother to confirm that this was the second contact with the same alien, but became alarmed when Ross informed her it was actually the third encounter. Jessica had not been aware that Ross had communicated with the alien again while on a solitary fishing trip in southwest Texas twenty years after the Moon encounter, but she was ready to hear all about it now.

After filling her in on all the details he knew about the alien species, Ross continued by claiming that the aliens had actually done the human race a favor. By informing us early about something that our own scientists would discover in due course, they had given us a tremendous opportunity to save additional lives. He concluded by adding, "What we need to decide is whether or not we should act on that knowledge!"

The walk back to the cabin was quiet and somber. The only question that Jessica asked her brother was if he intended to discuss the current topic with Patty. He told her that wasn't the best idea just yet, because Patty had been telling him to keep quiet about his belief in extraterrestrial life since he built the model of the solar system sixty years before back in Rumley.

Although Jessica understood his point, she also understood that his wife deserved to hear the information first hand as opposed to a leak via the media. Jessica asked her brother if the two of them could please have a quiet conversation with Patty before meeting with a science team. It was important that Patty be brought into the loop, and Ross nodded positively to her because deep down he knew she was right.

# 38

## *To tell, or not to tell*

Early the next morning Ross took another long walk through the woods to mull over the most important question of his life, as he needed to decide if he should inform the world of this new found knowledge or not. An argument could be made for both sides of the equation, but what would serve the most good? If he withheld the information the citizens of the world would have less time to prepare for the unavoidable impact of the asteroid, but they could all continue, be they happy or not, with their current structure of life. Babies would be born, young people would fall in love, people would go to work and enjoy their leisure time, and the bills would be paid all in the cover of blissful ignorance, but was that ultimately fair?

That question in itself brought forth an additional debate as some would claim they were better off not knowing about their probable demise, while others would want to know so they could spend as much time with loved ones as possible. Ross knew the information could cause a global panic that would manifest itself in a variety of ways including anarchy, but that panic would take place anyway once the astronomers discovered the problem and their findings somehow leaked out through the media.

At some point the military forces of the world would get involved, and it wouldn't matter if they had roughly twelve or eighteen months to work with. They would claim that they could rectify the situation by blasting the object out of the sky with a barrage of "who knows what" that would turn it into rubble. Unfortunately that option was probably more of a Hollywood solution, and not very realistic. Still, it would be foolish to not explore that course of action when push came to shove, as any possibility to save the planet would certainly deserve some level of consideration.

If Ross decided to release the information, he would have to explain in detail how he was privy to such devastating knowledge. Ross knew that when he informed the media about his now third contact with an alien species, the vast majority of people around the world would simply not believe him. Many would doubt his mental stability, and therefore his validity as the so called "Leader of the Free World". That would seriously jeopardize his ability to help with possible solutions, because all the non-believers would want him placed in a padded cell.

There would be serious religious implications around the globe as well, because many people of deep faith cannot fathom the thought of the Earth not being the focal point in the grand scheme of the universe. Ross of course knew differently, and there had been many times during his life when he wanted to convince religious fanatics that their belief system was not of sound logic. If God indeed had the ultimate power to create everything, then why would this planet be his only petri dish? It was a mathematical impossibility that humans were alone in the incredible unknown vastness of space, but people needed to believe in their core foundation. According to what the aliens had told Ross on the Moon during his first contact with them, their species had discovered, and then observed, some sort of life in roughly twenty percent of the solar systems they had explored. They had also admitted to him that they had only charted a small section of all that was out there.

There was no question in Ross' mind that the events of the next eighteen months and beyond would shake some of the core religious beliefs of many people on planet Earth, but he couldn't afford to get off on that thought process at the present time. He also knew that Patty wouldn't believe him about the aliens, and that was disconcerting because he would need her standing at his side throughout all the ridicule he would undoubtedly receive.

When Ross returned to his cabin, a staff member informed him that Jessica had gone to the main cabin for some coffee. Ross joined her on the quest and after sitting together in uncomfortable silence for a few minutes she asked him if he had decided what to do when they got back to the White House. Ross nodded positively, but asked his most trusted advisor, "What are your thoughts?" before revealing his decision. Without any hesitation Jessica said, "As President of the United States it's your duty to inform the public as soon as possible. You must gather a well accredited science team first, because in my opinion that would be the prudent thing to do!" She then added "If they believe you and your story, then the extra six months would help the brain trust of the planet come up with possible survival solutions." Ross nodded positively again, and then stated, "It's a difficult situation to be sure, and I have made my decision."

While on his solitary walk, Ross came to the conclusion that all of the reasons for withholding the information were outweighed by the reasons for releasing it. Ross knew it would be impractical to attempt keeping something of this magnitude a secret, and he, or any other world leader for that matter, didn't have the right to play God by doing so.

# 39

## *Secret in the closet*

The Marine One helicopter carrying Ross, Jessica, and his secret service detail touched down in customary fashion upon the south lawn of the White House. A small contingent of the media was typically waiting nearby for him, and Ross smiled and waved to them as he strode confidently by. He knew it was all part of the pomp and circumstance associated with the job, but wondered just how many times during his presidency did they need to film him emerging from the helicopter? Then he thought to himself that armed with the news he would soon reveal to them, and the world, it might be the last time they filmed him in such a lighthearted moment.

When greeted on the lawn by one of his aides, Ross asked her to locate the first lady and request that she please meet him and Jessica in the residence. A few moments later, Patty arrived at their bedroom to find Ross pacing back and forth, while Jessica stood quietly near the window. Patty gave Ross a hug and a gentle kiss before asking him how Camp David had been, and he responded by saying, "It had been incredibly educational!" That brought forth a rather quizzical look from his wife, but she moved over to greet Jessica as Ross moved towards and then opened the door to the hallway.

He spoke briefly with his most trusted sentry who was posted outside, and made it abundantly clear to him that he was not to allow anyone to get past him unless the world was coming to an end. After hearing "Yes sir Mr. President", Ross closed the door and began to quietly laugh at himself because of the irony of his statement. He then asked the two ladies now seated on the couch to follow him into the huge closet area. The expression on Patty's face then turned from quizzical to one of concern, but she complied with Ross' request.

Over the course of the next thirty minutes, Ross very quietly spilled his guts to Patty about what had really happened on the Moon thirty-five years before, the events of his fishing trip to Texas twenty years later, and the most recent contact while at Camp David the previous day. Ross also spoke of the conversation with his father Robert on his death bed, and what had been told to both Ross and Jessica about their mother Janet's supposed abduction.

When he was all finished, Patty looked at them both intently for a few minutes and then began to laugh out loud. She asked them how long it had taken the two of them to put this practical joke together, while also giving them credit for their collective imagination. Ross responded by saying, "It was no joke, and every bit of what he had just told her was true." Patty glanced over at Jessica and asked, "Do you really believe this ridiculous fabrication, or did you actually see the alien at Camp David?" Jessica stood by her brother and said, "Even though I did not see the alien, I believe everything that Ross has said." Patty began to laugh again, and said, "The two of you are daft if you really believe in aliens or abductions." Ross then informed her that the plan was to get a science team from around the globe together, and discuss it with them before going public with the information.

At that point Patty took a step back and said, "This joke has gone on far enough!" Ross looked deep into her eyes and reiterated, "This is all true, and someday soon I will be able to prove it to you." Patty returned the deep look into his eyes, and realized he actually believed everything he had just told her. She reminded him that he had been ridiculed in grade school back in Rumley for believing in extraterrestrials, and had seriously jeopardized his career back in Austin when he had talked with his assistant Mrs. Remington about it. Ross had been lucky that she was so loyal to him while he was in the State House of Representatives and then the Senate, but more importantly that she had kept her mouth shut all these years.

Patty enlightened her husband by telling him that the real reason that Mrs. Remington had not stayed on his staff and moved to Washington D.C. when he was elected to the United States Senate was because of his belief in alien life. She didn't think that Ross should be in national office with that potential mental instability, but she had kept quiet about it. She, along with most of the world, would probably think Ross was crazy to believe all that he had just revealed.

Ross informed Patty that he had thought through all of that, but the needs of the people of the planet far outweigh his own vanity. There was now a very strong possibility that no more history books would be written to discuss his legacy as a political figure, and Ross had no more elections to win even if there were. Public opinion only mattered in the sense of how Ross would be able to assist with any plans to help save as many people as possible.

He continued by saying, "Most people will think it's crazy, but there will be some believers that will take precautions to try and live through the awful event that will take place in eighteen months." In conclusion he stepped even closer to his wife and said, "By the time we all get halfway through that time

181

frame, the astronomers of the world will have conclusive evidence that what I revealed about the asteroid and the impact is true. That's when all hell will break loose, because the denial won't save them. My good name will be restored once again, but that will mean nothing if people don't take action!"

Unfortunately for Ross, his rant had fallen on deaf ears. Patty just refused to believe in anything that he had just told her, and was very surprised that Jessica had been taken in and was now a willing participant in the outlandish tale. It had been the one aspect of their long relationship that was a source of anguish, and Ross knew that the only way Patty would ever believe in alien life was if she actually had contact with one. He also knew that he would never have to worry about her becoming a security problem, because Patty wouldn't risk her current lifestyle or social standing by discussing what he had just told her.

# 40

## The initial plan

The first step in the process of putting together a team was to consult with his own National Science Advisor about the challenging problem at hand, and ensure that he understood the importance of keeping the news a complete secret. Ross instructed his advisor to quietly contact a group of global astronomers who possessed the advanced credentials necessary to be of use, but also the ability to keep quiet about the content of their discussions. The scientists would need to have an open minded approach to discuss the validity of such an asteroid impact, but also present viable possible solutions to help people survive the ordeal.

Roughly a month later the group assembled in a cabin at Camp David, and was then shocked to see the President of the United States walk into the room. At that moment Ross knew that his National Science Advisor had done an excellent job of not only getting the group of individuals to assemble by taking a break from their respective research projects, but had also kept his name out of the purpose of the conference.

As the meeting progressed Ross fielded all the questions that came from the panel, but was admittedly lost when it came to some of their collective technical vocabulary. As a former astronaut, Ross understood more of what the group was discussing than most politicians would have, but was intelligent enough to know that he wasn't the smartest person in the room. Ross was relieved that the group not only believed the information that he had put forth to them, but that they were already brainstorming to find possible solutions to the problem. That was not a new concept to this group of scientists, as most astronomers have known for many years that a multitude of objects have impacted the Earth's surface since long before mankind's arrival. What made this discussion different for the entire room was that the knowledge of this impending impact had been provided to the President of the United States by an alien species. One esteemed astronomer from Australia even asked Ross if the alien had alluded to the overall size of the asteroid, but Ross was unable to provide such potentially critical data.

Back at the White House, Jessica was preparing for the next phase of the plan that she had helped Ross develop. After his return from Camp David, Ross would meet with the Joint Chiefs that represented each branch of the military, the directors of Homeland Security, the CIA, DOD, FBI, and a few others in the secure basement bunker of the White House. He would instruct them all to keep the information in strictest confidence until otherwise notified, but wanted each of them to start developing plans that would help keep the peace when the panic and chaos began. Ross knew martial law would be inevitable at some point before the impact of the asteroid, but he also hoped to keep things in America somewhat normal for as long as possible.

A few weeks after that meeting, Ross would then request a closed door session of the United Nations assembly in New York City to address the delegation. His plan was to speak individually with the representative delegation of as many countries from around the world as possible before standing in front of the main body, so he could get a sense of how the news would be received. The hope was that each of the delegates would quietly get the word of the impending problem back to the leading member of their countries' government, and then the leaders of the world could work together in a beneficial way with the limited time available to help save at least a fraction of the human race.

It was a huge security risk without a doubt as some of the delegates would probably laugh in the face of the President, but it seemed the best way to get the information out globally. Ross and Jessica both knew that within minutes after the announcement the media would run with the story. It was inevitable that someone in the United Nations would leak the news, and that was not only something that couldn't be avoided, but it was somewhat necessary. A large contingent of media would be positioned at the United Nations building, as was nearly always the case, but this time they would have the story of all stories.

# 41

## *Ripples and rebounds*

As had been predicted, the news of President Ross Martin's shocking address to the United Nations general assembly spread like wildfire. It was now mid-April and a full six weeks had passed since his last encounter with the alien, so Ross informed the world that he believed the asteroid would impact sometime during August of 2022. That was only sixteen months away, and there was a multitude of decisions to be made, and projects completed, before that time expired. Ross had no proof to back up his claim other than the word of the alien species and his own as an honest man, but asked the people of the United States, and the world, to have faith in his prediction.

Unfortunately it would be difficult to gain the peoples trust in this particular instance for two reasons. Firstly, due largely in part to the influence of movies, television, and the internet, the thought of alien life actually helping the human race instead of being a hostile and invading force was beyond most people. Secondly, at least in America, the media had done such a tremendous job over the previous half century of misleading the citizens into false fear, that they had become numb to the thought of another cataclysmic event. Although there were a multitude of examples of that persuasive conduct, a few hugely significant events instantly came to mind for Ross. The cold war with the Soviet Union no longer existed, but the media had a field day with the hype of, "The Russians are coming!" for decades during the conflict. The "Y2K scare" at the turn of the century had turned out to be nothing at all, because the computers throughout the world kept functioning. The "Weapons of mass destruction" that supposedly existed after the attacks of September 11, 2001 had in fact been fabricated as a way to scare the American people into backing a foreign war, and the media fueled the flames of that fear whenever possible. Finally, the Mayan calendar had reached the end of its most recent cycle in December of 2012, but the world didn't come to an end as many had predicted. On a much smaller scale, the American media had even treated a winter storm as the potential end of days in some cases.

Ross knew that everything the media did was based on sensationalism and the next big story, and now they would go after him. He felt quite sure that the spin of his announcement would be that the President of the United States had gone beyond the edge of reasonable thought, because that would sell the most copy and advertising. It was indeed pathetic, but the reality of the modern world media.

Patty was correct in her assessment that Ross' name and reputation would be dragged through the mud. His open admission to not only the belief in, but actual contact with, extraterrestrials on three separate occasions had damaged his image. The media was certainly less than kind to the President of the United States, and the Congress began to have serious doubts in Ross' leadership abilities. On the positive side, there were people from various areas of the planet who believed his story, but they seemed to be few and far between.

Soon after his announcement the numbers associated with the New York Stock Exchange such as the DOW and the S&P 500 began to slide downwards, and by mid-June of 2021 they resembled those that had not been seen since the late stages of George Bush's presidency in 2008. Most Americans, whether they wanted to publicly admit it or not, were driven by money more than anything else, so with the dramatic downturn in the economy they began to lose faith in Ross as well. By the time the country celebrated its birthday on the fourth of July, Ross' approval ratings had plummeted to the point of reversing his seven to three victory margin during his re-election of only eight months before.

Life in the White House had become very difficult for Ross as well, because he knew that most of the staff was talking about him behind his back. They showed a measured amount of respect towards him as the current Chief Executive, but they now had little regard for the man. Very little was accomplished in the way of policy, because many in the legislative branch of the government were discussing the possibility of Ross' impeachment. Ross was safe for the moment in that he hadn't broken any federal laws, but the twenty-fifth amendment to the constitution could be invoked if he was found to be mentally incapacitated. To that end, Patty pleaded that Ross give up his crazy notion and return to the sane and stable man that she had known and loved for sixty years, but he would not yield.

As the calendar turned to August, even Jessica began to waver slightly in her belief of Ross. She had always been his most loyal and staunch supporter throughout their entire life, but the external pressure from seemingly everyone around her was beginning to take its toll. She had part of the equation from their father's story while he was on his death bed about their mother's abduction, but she had not seen the alien that Ross had spoken of.

Jessica began to wonder if Ross had somehow become delusional on the Moon when something had happened to Dennis, and had then parlayed the entire experience into some elaborate ruse. Had their father's story of the events of Roswell in 1947, and then the abduction in 1957, become the catalyst to spur on Ross' vivid imagination? Did Ross have such a strong emotional tie to Grandpa Hank that he would do whatever it took to justify his story of how the emblem and necklace had originated? For that matter, was her mother Janet accidentally, or intentionally, killed by her father Robert while on their overnight getaway? Had it been planned all along so he could get rid of her without anyone ever finding out? Did he bury her in the Texas desert, and make up the entire story of the car accident before changing that into an alien abduction?

The final few questions made Jessica realize that her imaginative thoughts were quickly getting away from her in a completely negative direction. She knew from how the family looked in the old black and white photographs that her parents loved each other very much, and it was foolish to think that her father would have ever hurt her mother. There was still the question of Ross though, and she needed to satisfy her curiosity. Jessica decided that the only way to deal with the situation was to stare Ross straight in the eye and demand the truth, but that might be the straw that broke his back. She knew that Ross needed to know he had his sister's faith more than anyone else's, so she would need to tread lightly.

The following day Jessica said good morning to Mrs. Patterson, and then tapped lightly on the door of the oval office before opening it. She found her brother busy as always at his desk and just concluding a phone call, so she stood quietly until he finished. When Ross hung up she said, "Can I have a minute of your time, because I need to say something to you that is very important." Ross replied, "I have something important to say to you as well, but ladies first."

Jessica took a deep breath and began by informing her brother in no uncertain terms, "I believe in you no matter what anybody else on the planet thinks, and I always will!" She admitted that she had gone through a brief period of doubting him during the previous few days, but some soul searching had convinced her once again that Ross was an honest man of true integrity. She concluded by adding "If you say there's an alien species that you have had contact with and they are trying to help the human race, then that's what I believe as well."

Ross stood to move around the desk so he could give his little sister a much needed hug. He knew that she had been constantly bombarded with negative words about him, but was proud of her for not folding under the pressure. Many people had underestimated her abilities over the years because of the leg brace, but Ross knew her resolve was nearly unmatched by anyone else he had ever met. He asked her, "Do you feel better now? If you are finished, then I'll tell you my important news." A nonverbal nod by Jessica confirmed that it was his turn, so he asked, "Can you guess who that was on the phone when you came in?" She shrugged while shaking her head from side to side, and then noticed Ross was smiling from ear to ear. Jessica hadn't seen him look like that for several months, so she begged him to fill her in. Ross said, "That was the National Science Advisor, and he was calling to inform me that during the last few hours several astronomers from around the globe had confirmed locating the incoming asteroid."

# 42
## *Joyous horror*

Jessica shouted with joy at the news, because she knew her brother would soon be vindicated by all his previous doubters. The asteroid had been discovered by astronomers just as Ross said it would, so there had to be truth in what he had been telling the people of the world all along. His critics, which literally numbered in the billions at this point, would have to eat crow for doubting him, but the joy of this particular victory would be bitter sweet.

It took Jessica about fifteen seconds to realize that the entire human race would have been better off if Ross had been delusional about the upcoming horrific event, because now they faced possible extinction. To both Ross and Jessica it seemed only fair that news of this magnitude should spread as quickly around the globe as his announcement back in April had, but they also knew there was much to discuss among other world leaders before the news could be released to the general public.

Just then, Mrs. Patterson knocked and moved through the door with a member of the secret service close behind her. She had heard Jessica shout, and they didn't know if something had happened to her, or the President. Finding both Ross and Jessica standing near the desk in no apparent danger or discomfort, she noticed that her boss was smiling from ear to ear. Wendy had now known and worked for Ross for nearly eighteen years, and had known Jessica even longer from their days at the law firm together in Houston. She was well accustomed to reading the mood of both of them, and she could tell something had made them both very happy. Based on Ross' current low point in popularity and faith from the American people, Mrs. Patterson surmised there could only be one cause for her boss's mood. She looked directly at his smiling face and said, "Can I assume someone has located your asteroid Mr. President?"

Within a few hours, Ross was back in the secure bunker under the White House with the Joint Chiefs. He wanted to find out what level of planning had been done by them all for the eventuality of the asteroid impact. Deep down Ross knew that none of them had believed him back in April when he directed them to come up with some ideas, but they were also very professional men who would have followed his orders whether they thought he was crazy or not.

As he had figured months before, the military boys had devised some system to try and blow the giant rock out of the sky. Their plan was to wait until the asteroid had moved into a position that was very close to the Earth, and then have all the nations of the world with sophisticated rocket technology fire everything they had at the object. They also informed Ross that they would of course hold back some of our nuclear arsenals in reserve, just in case a rogue nation decided that was a perfect time to launch an attack on the United States.

Ross thanked them for the input, and said it could be a consideration as a last ditch effort. He also informed them that their plan was limited in scope because a vast majority of the world's nations could not help with the endeavor due to a lack of said sophisticated rocket technology. He concluded by adding that those few nations that did in fact have the necessary technology would probably surmise that we would hold back, and they would therefore inherently want to do the same. It seemed to Ross that with that mindset, the Earth would be throwing only half a nuclear effort towards a giant rock in space that could possibly destroy the planet. What made it even more ridiculous, was that we would be holding back on the effort because we still needed a way to destroy each other in the event that the asteroid didn't.

The leading military minds of the nation literally wanted to sit on their hands until the last few days before impact, and then hope their plan would work. Ross believed it was an insane thought process, but was well aware from his military background that it was somehow justified in the minds of the men with the stars on their shoulder boards. There had been no mention by the generals of an alternative plan to prepare for the worst in the event that blowing the asteroid to bits didn't work, and that was not good news.

Next in line to discuss their options were the folks who worked at places with initials to identify them like the CIA, DOD, and FBI. Their collective thought process seemed to be centered on saving only the Americans, as if that particular sect of global society was somehow more deserving than others. To narrow the scope further, they intended to incorporate blue collar labor to somehow provide the more affluent white collar citizens, including themselves, with shelters to "ride out the storm".

Ross couldn't believe what he was hearing. He stood to move about the room, as he loudly boomed out his opinion of disappointment towards their collective myopic solutions to what was a global concern. The only aspect of what had recently been conveyed to Ross that made any sense at all was the word "shelters". That would undoubtedly be the key to the survival of the human species, but the parameters of such an undertaking would need to be defined more clearly before they could move forward. As Ross continued to circle the room, he began to discuss the thought of shelters with the assembled group. It seemed to be a sound approach to the problem at hand, and it needed to be discussed at greater length with other world leaders. There may be other possible solutions, but building shelters could provide some of their respective citizens with a fighting chance at survival.

After returning to his chair at the head of the long conference table, Ross made it quite clear to the Joint Chiefs that they all needed to start coming up with some sound ideas in a hurry. He knew they had collectively been caught somewhat off guard by this meeting, because they never believed in the asteroid or the aliens to begin with. Before dismissing them all from the room, Ross used his most stern tone when he said, "I really don't care if any of you believe me about the alien species now or not, but you all better start thinking about the asteroid more seriously!" Although unsure of the exact date of impact, he knew that the Earth as they all knew it only had a year at the most.

# 43

## *Global denial*

News of the discovery spread like a wild brushfire with the ever present fanning from the media. Soon everyone in the world who wanted to know about the asteroid could find out what little was known about it at the present time. All of the leading scientific teams throughout the world were now locking in on the asteroids position so they could attempt to learn more about it. The most important information to ascertain would be the trajectory of the rogue object, as well as the overall size and composition. If the astronomers could confirm that it was indeed on a collision course, then how large the rock was could help them determine the possible catastrophic damage it would cause. Next would be attempting to determine the date of impact, but that would only matter if collision was imminent.

In spite of a steady diet of spoon feeding throughout the previous half century via television and movies of the possibility of extraterrestrial life visiting Earth, the vast majority of the American citizens thought the announcement of the asteroids discovery was nothing more than a well-orchestrated hoax. Many people had lost a tremendous amount of faith in the government over the years due to being lied to during such events as the Watergate Scandal, or the misguided extreme expense of a "War on Terror" to name a few. Each of those examples, and many others by individuals or groups of people, had brought shame to the United States in one form or another when it was discovered how much deception was involved. Some Americans believed the recent announcement was designed to provide the President with a way to "wiggle off the hook" for his outlandish claim of having met and communicated with an alien species. Many nations of the world felt that was true, but that it was also a ploy to make America look good in the world view once again. It was not beyond the realm of possibility that there wasn't even an asteroid hurling in our direction, but just another lie by a fearful government that was well known for misrepresentation at times.

Ross knew it would probably be sometime before the results of the astronomers' inquiries came in, but he had little doubt of what they would reveal. If there wasn't an impending problem, then why would the alien species bring it to his attention to begin with? With that in mind, he began to make plans for saving as many of the world's population as possible.

His first step was to prepare a written proposal that he would then have translated and dispatched to all the heads of government around the world. After that, he would speak with whoever would listen to him about the construction of shelters. Ross knew that he needed to attempt what would be a tough sell to almost everyone in the world with the exception of the global scientific community, and he would probably receive some additional grief for doing so.

It seemed logical to sculpt out large cave structures in order to house the people and supplies that would be necessary for a potentially long duration of time. It also seemed that the best places to have those shelters would be in the mountains of as many different countries around the globe as possible. The scientific teams probably wouldn't be able to pinpoint where on the Earth the asteroid would impact until shortly before the event, so having multiple supposed safe havens just seemed like a prudent move. Ross could visualize literally hundreds of large caves within the Andes Mountains that stretched for a few thousand miles near the western edge of South America, or lower sections of the mighty Himalaya Mountain Range of Asia. There were of course many other suitable locations in mountain ranges such as the Alps in Europe, which could handle the needs of large population centers throughout the world.

As far as North America was concerned, the western half of the continent offered more, but not all of, the best mountainous options. In the United States, the general area of the continental divide along the Rocky Mountain range from Montana on down to New Mexico could prove quite useful, while closer to the west coast the Sierra Nevada and Cascade ranges would also be viable options. Additional fortifications could be located in the smaller western ranges of the Sawtooth or Wabash, while the Appalachian, Allegheny, and Adirondack Mountains could pick up the slack for the northeastern quadrant of the country.

If this proposal was to be globally accepted as a viable course of action, a tremendous amount of international cooperation would be necessary. Some countries of the world have the majority of their land very close to sea level, so those citizens might need to use the caves built in another country. Even if they could construct caves of their own, they might not be as safe as ones built at higher altitudes.

The odds were in favor of an ocean impact because roughly seventy percent of the Earth's surface consisted of water, and the series of massive waves that could be caused by such an impact might flood out any low lying caves. That scenario held true for certain areas of America as well, because many of the states along the gulf coast and lower eastern seaboard had little or no mountains to speak of.

While Ross verbally spelled this all out, and Mrs. Patterson put it into the computer, he suddenly flashed back to a conversation he had years ago with Dennis Strickland. Ross asked Mrs. Patterson to remind him to give the Strickland family in Colorado a call as soon as they were finished with the task at hand, because he needed to ask them for some information. Ross couldn't remember the exact amount, but he knew the family owned a significant amount of property within the state. He also remembered how Dennis had told him that much of it was located at high elevation.

When Mrs. Patterson asked him if there was anything else he wished to add to the current proposal, Ross quickly snapped back to the reality of the moment. He continued by saying it would be important that any and all occupants of the caves must have some sort of useful function. By that he meant that some people would be needed to build the shelters by blasting away the rock, and they would also be needed to help maintain the structural integrity of the caves. Others would be responsible for the growing and harvesting of food sources such as plant life or animals. Another group would need to hunt whatever animals were available in the wilderness near the caves during the last few weeks before the collision, and have that meat ready for consumption by the masses when they moved underground.

Beyond that there would be a need for people to gather, ration, and distribute the water supply available to each cave. There would also be a need for people to do cooking or cleaning, while others with the necessary education would be responsible for the sanitation issues of transforming human waste into useable topsoil and fertilizer for crops. Each shelter would also need to have doctors and nurses to take care of any medical issues that would most certainly arise. Perhaps the one bright spot in this entire proposal was that there probably would no longer be any need for lawyers, but Ross wasn't going to confront Jessica with that thought just yet.

The entire process hadn't yet taken into account the skills needed to create available access to the shelters throughout the world. Each host country would need to build roads and trails to the entrance points for multiple reasons. Aside from getting the people into the shelters, there needed to be a way for all the animals, food, water, and other supplies to be shuttled in. That could entail building some small bridges in difficult to reach areas, and time was growing short for that type of work.

No matter what the distinct duty assigned to each person might be everyone involved would need to work together in some level of harmony. It was necessary in order for the shelters to accomplish their intended task. There was a possibility that the occupants might need to live inside the caves for many months, or years, just to survive.

It would be impossible to accurately predict before the asteroid collision how extreme the atmospheric conditions might be, but conventional wisdom suggested that thick dust and huge debris clouds could envelop the planet after the collision. That would be a byproduct of an impact on land, or a large enough one in shallower areas of an ocean, but in either case venturing outside would become detrimental to ones' well-being. There was plenty of evidence throughout history to validate such scientific claims, with several volcanic eruptions at various locations around the planet during the previous century alone. The plume ash clouds of such events had caused many nearby inhabitants to protect themselves against the accidental inhaling of the dangerous substance that could cause severe respiratory problems. Plant and animal life were negatively affected as well. One volcanic event had taken place in the Pacific Northwest region of the United States when Mount St. Helens erupted in 1980. That event created a massive river of mud and debris such as fallen pine trees that tore through the adjacent mountainside, and scattered ash a few inches deep on some of the nearby towns.

Environmental conditions from an asteroid impact eventually would allow people to venture outside again, but until then, all food would need to be grown indoors. That would be a hugely important task that would require special training, and Ross would need to consult with some of the leading agricultural minds of the country to formulate and implement such a plan.

On the back end of the entire stay within the caves there would once again be a need for those people who specialized in hunting and gathering. When the surviving populace begins to emerge, new sources of food and water would need to be located. There may not be any animal life left to speak of on the surface, but whatever there was would need to be hunted for continued survival. New areas to grow crops would need to be located near whatever water sources might exist, which had just become an additional reason for locating the shelters at high elevation. If and when the atmosphere began to produce snow and rain again in an attempt to cleanse the planet, that water would need to be captured for use from the mountain runoff.

Global communications would most probably no longer exist in terms of what mankind is currently used to, so at first the inhabitants of neighboring caves would have to resort to the archaic form of face to face communication. That was sure to have a shocking impact upon many who had become overly accustomed to having communication and information access to the world in the palm of their hand. Those people would soon realize that it was significantly less important in the big picture to be informed, as opposed to being alive.

There was of course the possibility that all of this advanced planning would be pointless because the asteroid could either miss the Earth entirely, or be large enough that it would be a total planet killer. If the later of the two were true, then all the planning in the world wouldn't matter. If however neither one of the two scenarios came to fruition, then at least the efforts of building and fortifying shelters would give some people an outside chance at survival.

With that Ross concluded his thoughts on the shelter proposal, and thanked Mrs. Patterson for preparing the document. It would take some time for the world leaders to get back to him on the subject, and for all he knew many of them were currently working on a similar plan of action. Ross knew that his current thoughts had only begun to scratch the surface of the potential logistical nightmare that lay in front of him and other world leaders, but he would welcome any additional constructive ideas. In essence the plan needed to be approved and put into action yesterday, because time was now something that could not be wasted.

Ross asked Mrs. Patterson if she could please get the information she had taken down out to the appropriate people for translation as soon as possible, and then place a call to the Secretary of Agriculture. Ross hoped that he would know the names of some brilliant minds in the field, and be familiar with any new technologies that could be helpful to the cause. As Mrs. Patterson headed for the door Ross had one more request of her, and instructed her to please place a call to the Strickland family in Woodland Park before she did anything else.

# 44

## *Reluctant acceptance*

By the time the autumnal equinox of September signified the passing of summer into fall within the northern hemisphere; a few more American citizens were beginning to accept the inevitable. Throughout much of the previous month, astronomers and scientific teams had focused a tremendous amount of attention onto the path of the asteroid. They had been able to ascertain that impact seemed imminent, and were now attempting to determine the overall mass of the object.

During the same time, Ross and other world leaders had begun to have a more open and meaningful dialogue with regard to what should be done about it. Many had now read through the proposal set forth by Ross, and a few had made some welcome additions to the overall plan. Construction was beginning to get underway on building shelters in caves throughout several mountain ranges in different regions of the world, but Ross knew enough to let other governments and countries develop their own systems of how to proceed.

In the United States, a sizable budget towards the efforts of the project had been approved by Congress, and Ross was hopeful that would encourage more people to get involved. Interviews were being conducted at hundreds of locations throughout the country to determine who was a candidate for the multitude of jobs such an undertaking would need for success. Unfortunately, the overall number of applicants was still rather meager. At first that was puzzling to Ross, because with each passing day more and more people seemed to believe that the impact of the asteroid was indeed going to take place. He knew that generally speaking, the culture of Americans was to almost blindly follow the hottest trend. In spite of all the posturing about individuality, Ross knew that most people wanted to fit in with a group somehow. Why then were they not following each other in droves to the interview locations for an opportunity to work for their own survival?

Suddenly the truth hit Ross like a brick, and he began to break the American citizens down into their respective groups or demographics. In time there would be a large demographic that would become dedicated to the project, which would not surprisingly grow in numbers as the time of demise grew near, but they had not yet formed. For the time being, most people were still trying to figure out which group would be the "coolest one" to hook up with.

Ross began with the senior citizens, to which he, Patty, and Jessica had somewhat reluctantly become. Ross didn't feel much like a senior citizen, because he was still both very healthy and active, but he nevertheless was part of that demographic. He tried to put himself into that collective mindset, so that he could further understand what those millions of people might think of the shelters.

It occurred to him that many of the elderly may simply want to live out their time that was left on Earth in peace and quiet. A large contingent of seniors may have lived in the same house for much of their lives, and therefore had no desire to go anywhere else. It was a safe bet that many had lost their spouse in recent years, and might look upon this as a noble way to join them again in the afterworld. To them all the hardship associated with relocating to, living in for who knows how long,

204

and then with vast amounts of luck emerging from the shelters to a world that would have very little if any resemblance to what they left behind was simply too much to handle. Certainly seniors would not be turned away if they possessed a needed skill set and wanted to participate, but Ross didn't expect many of them to do so. In general, that demographic could not be looked down upon for their thought process, but serious dedication to the shelters was probably not a priority to them.

There would be one huge demographic that would span all ages, and that would be the religiously devout. Ross admired anyone who had developed and maintained a belief system in whatever had given them inner peace, but he also knew that some had taken that passion to another level. Many people would stand firmly behind their God of whatever religion they practiced, and Ross had no intention of trying to sway them away from their devotion.

Millions within the United States, and in other parts of the world, would believe to their core that it was part of God's master plan to save them from the peril of the asteroid, but Ross had no right or power to condemn them for it. After all, he believed with all his being in the existence of extraterrestrials, and many felt that was crazy. The only difference between the two was that Ross had actually come face to face on a few occasions with an alien, but he didn't know anyone who could actually claim to have met God. It was not a subject for debate that Ross intended to get into with anyone, because it would most probably end badly, but it was interesting to think about. Ross realized that in spite of the words often spoken of, "Love and help thy neighbor", many of the religious faithful would also stay in their homes without an interest in the shelters.

Moving to the opposite end of the scale, Ross knew there would also be a demographic that would be much more dangerous. Without actual confirmation, he knew there were probably already a large amount of people that had become "panic movers". Those were the individuals or families that had taken everything upon themselves for survival. They would have packed up whatever they deemed to be most precious into their cars, and made a run for the hills. Many would then fall victim to outrageous price gouging by those they met along the way who could provide goods or services to what would obviously be desperate people.

The lucky few would find a cave or something similar, and then defend it with everything they had. That demographic was dangerous because there would be theft of supplies needed for their own needs, and that would inevitably lead to violence in order to obtain or protect the supplies. They would be acting as individuals instead of taking part in a team effort, and eventually the strain would probably become too much for them to handle. If small bands of these people did somehow unite, they would become even more dangerous as vigilante groups. That could cause a threat to the people who were fortifying the shelters with supplies, and Ross would need to convey that to other world leaders. It now seemed most prudent to have armed military personnel escorting any supply vehicles in the future, and guards posted at the shelter entrances to protect what had been stored.

Another demographic to consider would be that of the financially affluent. There would be many among that set of people who, out of nothing more than habit, would feel a natural entitlement to a place within the shelters. Although some had worked hard during their life to gain their fortunes, the majority had simply inherited the wealth. Even those who had earned their own way, probably had never done much, or any, of the physical labor associated with what would be needed to maintain the shelters. Ross could visualize a bidding war from certain members of that demographic at the entrances to the shelters, as they would wave stacks of cash in the face of the guards to gain entry. Of course he knew that would not be true for all of them, because with this, or any other sect of society, there would always be exceptions to the rule.

Unfortunately that same sense of entitlement would probably be seen within many of the elected officials at both the national and state levels. While some, like Ross, had come from humble beginnings, many had become accustomed to the comfortable financial lifestyle that their positions provided for them. Ross couldn't really fault those individuals, because he had also fallen into that trap during his many years of public service to the nation. Sadly, the line of who gained automatic entry to the shelters would need to be drawn somewhere.

Ross and his entire Cabinet, several leading members of the federal government, and all of their families had been guaranteed a place deep within the Colorado mountainside fortification of the North American Aerospace Defense Command, or NORAD. However, most other elected officials would be left to fend for themselves. It occurred to Ross that although his group would be kept in America's most secure underground location for the sake of maintaining the constitutional chain of succession, it would be wise to disperse the remaining members of Congress and state Governors to multiple shelters. That would increase the probability of at least some of them surviving, while at the same time providing a built in leadership role within each of the shelters throughout the nation. Ross would also need to make it clear to his own family, and to the entire aforementioned group, that this gift of automatic entry came with a price. Each one of them would be required to set the proper example for everyone else in the shelters by working hard at their given tasks to help ensure order and harmony.

The final major group of American citizens would be those who took the entirety of the situation seriously. They would be the people who interviewed for various labor positions, and then did their part by working hard to build or fortify the shelters. Once inside the shelters they would also work to maintain a harmonious lifestyle as best as could be expected, while everyone waited for a hopeful emergence. As Ross thought through all of this, it became obvious to him that this demographic would be the most important, but he hoped it wouldn't be the smallest.

With reluctant acceptance, Ross ultimately realized that the number of people in the United States who would be helpful to the cause of building, fortifying, and maintaining the shelters were vastly outnumbered by those who wouldn't. He also knew that something needed to be done in order to properly identify and protect those who were helpful, so he asked Mrs. Patterson to please place a call to the Surgeon General.

# 45

## A well-deserved gift

With the unmistakable tune created by toasting with fine crystal still lingering in the air, Ross and Patty each took a sip from their champagne glasses. Then they raised their glasses towards the rest of the assembled crowd within the White House, and wished them all a Happy New Year. The blizzard conditions over the past few days had not deterred anyone on the guest list from attending the celebration to usher in 2022, but this was not the normal crowd to attend such an event.

During the fall, Ross and Patty had decided to host this party for each and every staff member of the White House and their families. Beyond some of the more recognizable faces, this group included those of gardeners, house keepers, cooks and servers. It was their way of saying thanks to each one of them for all the hard work and dedication they had shown over the course of the previous five years, and also a way to provide them all with a gift, and honor, they would never expect.

The previous three months had been filled with all sorts of activities for Ross and the family. Like multitudes of other people around the planet who had now accepted the inevitable, Ross had taken the opportunity to do a few things that would soon no longer be available. In October he had gone to historic old Wrigley Field in Chicago to throw out the first pitch for game one of the World Series between the Cubs and the Kansas City Royals. Ross thought it was nice for the fans of Chicago to have the Cubs finally win the big prize after several decades of frustration, but was saddened that it may have been the last of the fall classics. During early December Ross had also attended the Army vs. Navy football game, which he had been able to do only a handful of times since graduating from the academy.

Immediately after the closely fought game, which Navy won by two points, Ross headed west because he had some serious business to attend to. He surprised many people over the course of the next ten days by visiting at least a dozen of the sites in the western mountain ranges where construction and early fortification on some of the shelters was feverishly underway.

The demographic who took the entirety of the situation seriously was beginning to grow in numbers, and they had made some good progress with their work. Much of the rock that had been blasted from the mountainsides to create the shelters had been used to fill in small nearby ravines, and had therefore helped create better routes for the roads leading up to the entrances.

Ross was proud of his Surgeon General for responding in such a positive way to the call from the White House in late September, and had expressed his gratitude to her on several occasions. She had the idea to implant those people who had been working on the shelters from the earliest days of the project with a microchip, and Ross had fully endorsed the plan.

Many of the people that Ross met with during his surprise visits had already been implanted with the microchip that would guarantee their place in the shelters, but he identified several more at each site during the visits that had earned the same consideration. The implant was a brilliant idea that had given this particular group of people comfort in the knowledge that they would not be forgotten by their government or country for their efforts.

The final stop for Ross on his western tour was at the Strickland family home in Woodland Park, Colorado. He wanted to ask them a favor, and Ross didn't feel it was the type of thing that could be handled with a phone call. While sitting in the same beautiful home that he had first seen when Dennis had been laid to rest, Ross spoke with a few relatives of his old friend. They had been some of the few that had believed his story about the asteroid from the very beginning, and had been constructing a massive shelter of their own on their property high in the nearby mountains. Ross informed them that he and his family would seek refuge in the nearby mountainside NORAD fortification, while some staff members would use a shelter within the Appalachians, but he was concerned for the well-being of many others at the White House.

The Strickland family had been to the White House on a few separate occasions by invitation of Ross and Patty, and had met some of the people to which he spoke of. Ross asked if he could impose on the Strickland's to help him out with his dilemma, as some of those dedicated people had not been assigned a shelter. The Strickland family put Ross' mind at ease, as they informed him they would be happy to provide a place in their shelter for any of the White House staff and their families who needed the help. They understood many of them had been unable to leave their current positions at the White House in order to help with the shelters, but also weren't part of the group that would be given automatic entry. Ross was now assured that the only thing those people needed to do was make their own way to the mountains of Colorado.

With that Ross breathed a sigh of relief, and promised that, at his personal expense, he would send additional supplies and food stores for the extra people to the Strickland shelter well in advance of the asteroid impact.

Upon his return to the White House, Ross located Patty to inform her that the visit with the Strickland's had been successful, and she too breathed a sigh of relief upon hearing the news. The two of them decided that perhaps the best way to inform all those who might be impacted, was to wait until their already planned staff party on New Year's Eve. They thought the event would be a wonderful venue to provide them all with the surprise gift. Ross then headed in the direction of the oval office, because he knew there would be a multitude of phone calls and several business issues to catch up on after being away for ten days.

Before digging back into all that was waiting for him on his desk, Ross stared at the emblem on Grandpa Hank's necklace that still hung from the small reading lamp for a few moments. It reminded him of how limited his power was in the really big picture of the galaxy, but it had also always been the thing that kept him centered and focused on whatever task lay in front of him. Ross knew he was doing all that he could with his limited power to save some of the people of Earth who wanted to be saved, but it just didn't seem to be enough in his own eyes.

A knock, and subsequent entry, by Mrs. Patterson at the door snapped Ross back into the present reality once again. She had a list of items to go over with her boss, but before she could begin he told her he had an idea. His plan was to shut down the work on the shelters for two weeks during the time of Christmas and New Year's, because Ross felt that all those people should be able to spend significant time with their families if they wanted to. This would probably be the last holiday season as they knew it, so the work could wait while everyone spent time with their loved ones. Ross also felt that if he didn't provide them with a break, they could all become burned out on the job before the shelters were finished. There would be a stretch drive during the final months that would need maximum effort, and if they all worked too hard now they wouldn't have the strength to go on when it was needed most.

Mrs. Patterson agreed it was a good idea, so Ross asked her to place a series of calls for him after she had gone over the items she wished to discuss with him. It would add a significant amount to the already long list of calls he needed to make, but he wanted to personally speak with the foremen at each shelter to make sure they understood his wishes.

After a few longer than usual days in the office catching up on lost time, Ross began to really focus on Christmas with the family. He knew that this would probably be the last time they could all enjoy the holiday together in the warmth and comfort of the White House, and he left it up to Patty to make sure everyone would be there for at least a few days.

# 46

## Helping hands unite

As the people of Earth, including those at the White House, flipped the pages of their respective calendars to March, a new realization set in. With less than six months remaining until the asteroid impact, there was added incentive to get things done. In the United States, agricultural output was at an all-time high, as farmers were no longer instructed to hold back on their planting or harvesting in favor of market conditions.

Every acre of fertile farm land within the country was being used to either grow the food to sustain the people's needs within the shelters, or to fatten up all the livestock that would be slaughtered for the meat or placed inside the caves for other resources such as milk and eggs. Many more citizens had also joined the ever growing demographic of those who wished to help build and supply the shelters, but some had refused the opportunity to have the microchip implanted.

What had surprised Ross, were the actions of the large religiously devout demographic. It had been reported that in many areas of the world this societal group had come out in huge numbers to assist with the daunting task at hand. In general, the group still wanted no part of seeking refuge within the shelters, but felt it was the humane thing to do by helping in any way possible. They still believed God was going to save them in the end, but lending a hand to others was all part of the master plan. Ross admired their devotion, freely admitted he had been wrong in his previous assessment of them, and was glad for all those who would benefit by having the extra help.

At that point there were two dozen caves in Montana, Wyoming, and Colorado that were considered completed in the structural sense and each could house a thousand people. In the Cascade and Sierra Nevada mountain ranges to the west another dozen were in the same stage of readiness, with a few dozen more nearing completion in several areas. The majority of all the shelters had been constructed with eastward facing entrances and ventilation shafts, because it was unknown how high, or how far inland, the giant waves from the nearby Pacific Ocean could be after the asteroids impact.

Each of the massive caves would still need to be fortified with bunk beds, blankets, and other important features such as generators for lighting systems before any food or water would be brought in, but at least the structures themselves were ready for the next phase of preparedness. The work thus far had not been easy for the crews who dug them out, as the winter in the western United States had been brutal up to that point. Access to the shelters along the makeshift roads had been challenging at times, but the workers had done a great job of overcoming the obstacle. The positive side to the heavy winter was that it created a vast amount of snow that would be collected as it melted, and stored within the caves for later use.

Construction in the caves within the smaller mountain ranges in the eastern section of the country was not as progressed, but those had been started at a later date. Ross, and the leading engineering minds behind the project, had always wanted to have as many caves as possible in the Rocky Mountains. They had the benefit of being not only a much higher mountain range, but they were also significantly further away from any of the world's oceans.

Workers throughout the country had become united in a way that Ross had never imagined. He was overjoyed to see it happen, but was still surprised by it. The history books revealed that the current resolve was similar to that of the days of World War II, when the entire country seemed to ban together in the common goal of defeating a foreign enemy. This was of course an even larger undertaking in the big picture because it was truly a global threat, and many of the people seemed to finally be understanding of that fact.

In what had been a difficult decision to arrive at, Ross was now faced with the task of informing the citizens of the United States of something they would not be happy to hear. In a televised address to the nation, he informed them that personal driving would become a thing of the past at the end of March. The nation's supply of fuel would be needed for all the farm equipment that would harvest the crops destined for the shelters, and the truck convoys that would be transporting the fortifications. Those same convoys were currently being used to transport the massive number of bunk beds and generators to those shelters that were ready, and they would continue to do so as other caves were completed. Logging trucks were bringing vast amounts of fallen trees to the closest shelters, so a supply of wood for heat and cooking could also be stored within.

Once all of the fortifications, including food and water, had been transported to the caves, the convoys of trucks would then carry whatever fuel supply remained for use by the generators inside. The final trip, with the help of hundreds of busses, would then be to carry the most precious cargo of all, the people, to the shelters, and park adjacent to the entrances for hopeful use after the event was all over.

As of the first day of April, children would need to walk or ride their bikes to school. Parents would need to prioritize what was truly needed with the use of their cars or trucks, and complete those tasks as of the last day of March. After that, people who still wanted to report for their respective jobs would need to find alternative means to get there.

Ross knew he was asking the American people to give up a large piece of their personal identity by not allowing them to drive anymore, but it needed to be done for the greater good. The OPEC nations had just announced they would be jacking up the price of oil again, as if they needed another reason, and Ross had emphatically stated to Congress that, "The new price levels were beyond ludicrous!"

It had been decided that the United States would purchase no more oil from the cartel after the end of March, and that would put a strain on the oil producing capabilities here in America. Ross knew it was a drastic measure, but the country had been held hostage by those vultures for more than half a century now. There had been rhetoric on Capitol Hill for the majority of that time frame about America gaining its energy independence, and Ross had been involved in some of those discussions, but no real significant steps towards that end had ever been taken. Now, like it or not, those steps had been thrust upon the nation. Ross wanted to grant America such independence, even if it would only be for the last few months before everything on Earth would drastically change.

Ross wondered why those nations really thought the best way to prepare for the problem at hand was to rape and pillage the entire world for a commodity that was not only finite, but would become completely worthless very soon.

What good would it do them to have all that cash buried in a hole in the sand, while a few thousand feet of water rushed uncontrollably over their heads?  As far as Ross was concerned, they were idiots with myopic thinking who would pay the ultimate price.  His desire was to create a new policy that the United States would no longer allow any of those people, who were responsible for the recent price hikes, entrance into the country.

Meanwhile, the Earth had now rotated far enough around the sun that the asteroid was no longer visible to all the astronomers on the planet surface who had been studying it since the day it was located.  Earth was very close to the same position that it had been when the alien had informed Ross of the impending doom, and it would be several months until the astronomers could fixate on the asteroid again.

Fortunately NASA, and other global space agencies, had launched several probes towards the menacing rock during the previous few months.  That was done in an attempt to ascertain vital information such as its overall size and composition, but it would be sometime before the probes telemetry would send back useful results.

# 47

## *Shifting classes*

On a glorious warm and sunny day in May, Ross found himself back at Annapolis to give the commencement address for the Naval Academy graduating class of 2022. One such graduate felt incredibly honored, as the President of the United States repeatedly glanced over in his specific direction during the proceedings. What he didn't know was that Ross was not looking at him so much, as he was looking at the chair to which the young man sat upon.

Ross had done the same thing five years prior when he had given the commencement address to the class of 2017 during the first spring of his presidency, as that was the location of his seat when he had graduated from the academy in 1972. Could it really have been fifty years, he thought to himself, since he threw his cap into the air while following the customary tradition of all Midshipmen upon graduation? In some ways it seemed like only yesterday, but it had indeed been a long and fulfilling journey since that day many years before. Ross felt saddened by the fact that this could possibly be the last group of stellar young men and women to graduate from the academy, and then realized that same sentiment should be applied to hundreds of colleges and universities throughout the country.

The day in Annapolis, along the shore of Chesapeake Bay, had been a pleasant and much needed diversion from many of the trials and tribulations that Ross now faced. Over the previous few weeks, there had been several reports of mass looting in many of the cities and towns throughout America. In response, with the urging of his Cabinet, and then the help of Congress, Ross had implemented an increased level of military presence in some areas to help keep the peace.

It was now approximately ninety days until the impact of the asteroid, but the leading scientific minds of the planet had only been able to narrow down the specific time to a four day window during the final ten days of August. The looting was a definitive sign that the downhill slide of humanity was beginning to take hold, and Ross knew it would only get worse. Everyday life had become quite challenging for many families who lived in rural areas, because the "no personal driving mandate" had now been in effect for roughly seven weeks. Those who lived in the cities had an easier time of getting where they needed to be, but there was also a growing faction of those who no longer cared about anything.

Another interesting event that seemed to be taking place in many areas throughout the country was that of relocation. Reports were coming in from the inner cities and suburban areas of thousands of homeless people relocating into the dwellings of those people who had left them vacant to build, fortify, and then seek refuge in the shelters. Although some neighbors in the more affluent areas complained bitterly to the local law enforcement about the intrusion into their protected and sanitary world, most just accepted the shifting of classes. In most cases the former homeless were not the ones responsible for any of the looting; they were just using an available space for a much needed upgrade.

Armed with some new information that had just been discovered about the incoming asteroid, Ross decided he would address the nation in a few days to cover the homeless situation, and give the people a progress report on the shelters. During the time leading up to the televised broadcast, he made his intentions well known to the members of his Cabinet and Congress. A new nationwide provision would be announced that allowed the homeless to remain in the places they had relocated to, and law enforcement would be instructed to leave them alone. There were much more important things for local police to monitor, and Ross knew that his other news would create some social unrest.

Ross thanked the American people for their collective hard work and sacrifices, and then presented them all with the newest round of bad news. It was difficult for him to relay such horrendous findings, but it had to be done. Although the asteroid wouldn't come back into view for several more weeks, the size and composition had now been determined by the probes and verified by the leading scientific minds around the world.

The hope was that the makeup of the asteroid would be soft rock that had very little mass, but the opposite was true. Large quantities of iron had been detected which would make it much more dense than the Moon, but that was only part of the problem. That density would be less likely to burn up as it entered the Earth's atmosphere, and the impact itself would have a much harder punch to it.

Ross then informed the people that the size of the asteroid was roughly one-tenth that of the Moon, which was itself about one-fourth the size of Earth. Knowing full well that knowledge of fractions had become a thing of the past for most Americans; Ross did the math for them. With the most serious tone he had ever used while on television, Ross spoke of the reality check that had just slapped everyone in the face. He leaned closer to the microphone on his desk in the oval office and said to his constituents, "That means the asteroid is a full one-fortieth, or two and a half percent, of the size of this precious little blue marble that we all live on!" To put that into proper perspective for everyone, he added, "That could easily be compared to the size of Australia."

In terms of size compared to other asteroids that had impacted Earth throughout millions of years, this thing was enormous. It was in no way a water balloon either, as this particular asteroid containing a high concentration of iron was like a Nolan Ryan fastball coming straight at the Earths head. The only difference between the two was that a batter might have a chance to duck out of the way of the baseball, but orbital mechanics of planets were considerably less flexible. He concluded his thoughts on the subject by saying, "The efforts of the shelters will now have to be stepped up to a new level, and we all have precious little time to work with!"

Suddenly everyone in his Cabinet and Congress understood why he was pulling local police away from the homeless situation; because it became evident they would indeed be needed to maintain order in other places. Before signing off, Ross apologized in advance to the American people for changes and restrictions to their everyday life that would undoubtedly occur over the next several weeks, and told them all he would speak to them again soon.

When the lights on the cameras turned off and he heard the words "and we're out" from the production crew, Ross punched the button on his phone to summon Mrs. Patterson at her desk in the next room. Within seconds she entered the oval office, and Ross stood to whisper instructions into her ear. He was calling an immediate meeting of his Cabinet, and he wanted them all in attendance within the hour.

The discussion of the group would center on two main topics. First would be the implementation of food rationing throughout the nations grocery outlets within the next week, as the recent news about the asteroid would undoubtedly create an additional increase in the new level of looting and hoarding. Along those same lines Ross also wanted to implement a level of martial law that would prevent price gouging by store owners. The military presence would ensure that everyone had a fair chance to purchase food and water regardless of their economic standing, and would also provide an added level of safety to the store owners themselves. Second on the agenda would be a discussion of the monetary system and its inevitable collapse. It would only be a matter of time before it took place, and then most currencies around the world would become nothing more than worthless scraps of paper.

Suddenly Ross felt the small piece of strange metal in his pocket get very hot, which compelled him to glance over at the emblem on the necklace hanging from the desks reading lamp. The alien had given him the small trinket at Camp David during their most recent of encounters when he had informed Ross about the impending asteroid. He had been informed that a drastic change in the objects temperature would signify that a non-stealthy public visit by the alien would soon occur. Ross had carried the item around in his pocket every day since then, but had never really expected it to change in temperature. Now it was so hot that it was becoming uncomfortable to the touch, and Ross needed to use the handkerchief in the breast pocket of his suit to remove the item and drop it on his desk.

The following morning Ross and Patty were awakened by a phone call from his White House Chief of Staff and within a minute after the call a secret service detail began pounding on their bedroom door. Patty groaned as she climbed out of bed, and moved towards the sanctuary of the bathroom before Ross allowed the team of agents to enter. They informed Ross that he needed to be escorted down to the secure bunker beneath the White House immediately, because there was an aerial threat closing in on Washington D.C. It was a slow moving target, but the trajectory of the object suggested it was headed very close to the White House. The military defenses had been unable to shoot it down, or even alter the course, because it seemed to weave away from anything that was aimed at it.

With that Ross looked at the bedside table to see the small metal object glowing brilliantly again as it had done on his desk the previous day, and informed the men he would not be going into the bunker. He knew they had a specific protocol to follow, but he assured them that anything that could weave its way through the defense perimeter of Washington D.C. at a slow speed probably also had the capability to get to the bunker if they so desired. No member of the secret service detail, or anyone else for that matter, had any way of knowing what was about to transpire, but Ross did. He was still in the dark as to the content of the upcoming meeting with his old alien friend, but it had become obvious to Ross that the object heading towards the White House was an alien scout ship.

As Patty emerged from the dressing area in comfortable jeans and her favorite University of Maryland sweatshirt, Ross was completing a phone call to the head of the security detail that protected the White House. He was informing them that the incoming object would probably attempt to land on the nearby lawn, and they were hereby ordered to allow it to do so. Prior to that conversation Ross had contacted the commander of the nearby armed forces that had been attempting to shoot the object down, and had ordered them to cease fire immediately. The general had not been happy to receive the orders, but he had no choice but to comply as the instructions had come directly from the very top of the chain of command.

A short time later Ross stood on the south lawn area of the White House, and waited for the door, or hatch, of the alien spacecraft to open. He was nearly completely encircled by the secret service for protection, but he somehow knew it wasn't necessary. He clutched the small metal trinket that the alien had given him at Camp David, which was now ice cold again, in his left hand, while leaving his right hand empty in preparation for a welcome handshake.

The assembled members of the media, which were located in their customary positions nearby, had been filming the spacecraft's every move since a few moments before it had landed. A few of them began to shout out questions in the direction of the President, but were then interrupted as the hatch opened. Ross smiled broadly and reached out his hand to welcome his old alien friend as he descended the ramp, and not a sound could be heard from anyone else who was witnessing the historic event.

Patty, who was watching from the relative safety of the upstairs balcony, stood with mouth agape in total shock and disbelief. She now realized that her husband had been telling the truth about the existence of the alien species all along, and he had kept his vow that he would someday prove it to her.

Ross listened intently to the thoughts of the alien, and occasionally responded verbally to his guest. Those who were witnessing the encounter could not understand what he was responding to, because the alien had not projected his thoughts into anyone else's mind but Ross. The private conversation now being witnessed by perhaps millions of people worldwide continued for more than twenty minutes, while those standing nearby remained silent. Then Ross pointed toward the spire of the Washington Monument and said, "Right next to that would be perfect", before he once again shook the hand of the alien.

# 48

## Deep water

While seemingly most of the entire planet had become mesmerized by the live television footage of the encounter between President Ross Martin and an unknown creature from some far away alien world, a vessel of tremendous size was beginning to rise from the depths of the southern Atlantic Ocean. Not a soul on Earth was aware of the spaceships existence until now, as it had been resting on the bottom in extremely deep water for well over two Earth centuries.

When the alien species had returned to this solar system after an absence of several Earth centuries to construct their small base on the Moon for another round of scientific observations, they had also placed the larger transport vessel in a well hidden spot on the planet surface. At that time, the dominant species of ₹-829-२ग़-3 didn't possess the technology to explore and map the deep ocean floor, so it was a perfect hiding place.

In much more recent times that technology became available to the people of Earth, so the aliens had been forced to leave the vessel where it was or risk detection by moving it. Secrecy for the aliens was no longer an issue though, as it became imperative that they remove the large spaceship from the planet surface before the impact of the asteroid.

Ross was perhaps the first person on Earth to learn of the larger spaceships existence, as his old alien friend had just informed him of it when they communicated on the south lawn of the White House. Among many other thoughts that were transmitted, the alien had informed Ross that the spaceship would soon emerge from the ocean depths, and rise into the sky. At that point someone was bound to notice the strange craft, or satellite systems would detect it, and word would spread quickly. The transport ship would first go to the far side of the Moon, so they could gather up equipment and personnel from their observation base. It would then ascend to a higher Earth orbit, and provide the location where a fleet of similar spaceships from the alien home world would rally up with her.

That was the moment in the conversation that Ross' jaw fell open, as the alien presented him with an amazing offer. It was limited in scope, but it would provide a miniscule portion of the human species with an interesting option. In what was to be a mind blowing opportunity to ensure that the dominant species of ₹-829-३ग-3, or Earth, would not become extinct, the aliens were prepared to relocate a small sample of them to another solar system. The twelve spaceships that would join the deep water vessel in orbit were due to arrive soon, and they would remain in that orbital position until shortly before the impact of the asteroid. At that time all but the deep water vessel would land on various areas of Earth to collect those who had been selected to venture on to the new world.

Ross stopped his old alien friend for a moment to quietly ask some very important questions. The first was the obvious one of how many people of Earth could the transport fleet relocate to the new world, which was quickly followed by the perhaps more important questions of how, and by whom, would those people be selected?

Throughout all of the time since the alien had informed Ross privately of the impending asteroid, they had been keeping an even more watchful eye on the activities of the planet. The aliens had indeed been intrigued at how some percentage of the global population had been working very hard in a determined effort to save their species from extinction. However, it had also been noticed that a substantially larger number had done absolutely nothing to help the cause, and therefore this offer would not be extended to those people.

The alien continued by informing Ross that only one other condition existed, but other than that they wanted no part in the selection process. It would be up to Ross and other world leaders to come up with some method of how to choose the lucky ones, but there was limited time to develop and implement said method. Each of the twelve transport ships could accommodate up to eight hundred people for the voyage, but the selected passengers would need to be at specific locations for pick up when the time came. Ross was then informed that the coordinates for eleven of the locations would soon be transmitted to him and those locations would not under any circumstances be altered. The final transport ship would be sent to pick up Ross and his family, along with others who would be going from the surrounding area, and Ross could choose the landing location.

Although honored to be automatically pre-selected by the aliens as one of less than ten thousand pilgrims in quest of the new world, Ross couldn't understand why he, or his family, deserved such preferential treatment. With the planet wide population now close to eight billion, the number of people who could relocate to a new marble in space represented slightly more than one one-hundredth of one percent. The alien informed Ross that his selection as one of the dominant species on this planet that must survive was their second condition to the overall offer. Ross didn't know it at the time, and had never been informed by the alien at either one of their subsequent encounters, but the second alien that he had helped to survive on the Moon many years before was the commanding officer of the alien that Ross had originally made contact with.

Ross was now learning that the alien who Dennis encountered was actually one of the highest ranking officials in their space exploration fleet stationed in this sector of the galaxy. That particular alien was responsible for allowing Ross to have his second encounter with the extraterrestrial species while on his fishing trip, and why the first alien had visited Ross again at Camp David.

In his reports to the home world, the high ranking alien official had notified them about the events that took place on the Moon of ₹-829-ʒʊπ-3, and the recent development of the dominant indigenous species of the planet itself. Several follow-up reports submitted during the next thirty-six planetary cycles around the host star stated that closer observation of the species had revealed significant progress both technologically and philosophically. The most recent of those reports had also informed the home world that the species could very well become extinct due to the impending asteroid collision. He had been able to persuade his superiors, and eventually the command council, that the dominant species of Earth was worthy of survival, and was then given permission to pursue a course of action that could make that possible. The alien informed Ross that the command council had also given his commanding officer the option to personally select a few of the species that would survive, and Ross was at the top of his list.

# 49

## A change of heart

By early August, nearly all of the people from various parts of the globe that intended to seek refuge within the vast network of shelters were either already in them, or very close to the entrances assisting with final preparations. In the United States and Canada, it was believed that nearly a quarter of a million people could be housed in the two hundred and fifty mountain shelters that had been completed and provisioned. Similar numbers were hoped to be saved within the Andes of South America, while reports from Europe and Asia were even more optimistic.

Ross had never toured any of the facilities outside of the United States, so he had no way of personally verifying the state of readiness that each continent claimed. He would just have to take their word for it, and frankly the hopeful survival of his own citizens within the borders of America had long before become his main priority.

To that end, there was a new concern for Ross. As was to be expected, many people in the country had begun to have a change of heart about their respective choices. A vast amount of citizens who never lifted a finger to prepare for the coming of the asteroid were now interested in saving their own neck. Ross knew it was basic human instinct to search for a way to survive, but that survival should not come at the expense of others. The people who would occupy the shelters had earned the right to do so, and Ross was determined to provide them with that opportunity. Most people understood that the entire process had actually been completely fair and unbiased with regard to selection, because it had nothing to do with a person's race, creed, religion, economic standing, or even sexual orientation. In short, if someone possessed a necessary skill set, a strong work ethic, and a belief that the shelters were the best option to survive the ordeal, then they had been implanted with the microchip to assure them a place within what they had labored to build. It was that simple, and in Ross' mind no one had the right to snivel about it.

In spite of that belief, there were countless numbers of people in America that were leaving their homes and heading up into the nearest mountain range, because it presented at least a chance to survive. Ross felt confident the same could be said in other parts of the world, but once again that was not his problem. Many would be peaceful in their initial intent and never attempt to make their way into one of the shelters, but there would be others that would cause trouble. Ross also knew that the military presence at the entrances needed to be intensified as a safety precaution, and had done so several weeks before in anticipation of the current situation.

There had been hope that another change of heart would take place, but Ross had been unable at this point to make that happen. On July 7th, the day that Ross turned seventy-two, there was the typical birthday celebration in his honor at the White House. The event was the final social gathering to be scheduled at the mansion before many of the staff would begin their trek to either their assigned shelters, or to join their families in what could be the final weeks of their lives. Ross had used that venue to speak to those assembled about the third option that had been presented on behalf of the alien species. He had hoped to convince several of them to join him on the travel through space in quest of the new world, but only a few had shown even a glimmer of interest. The truly sad part was that he didn't have Patty's support when he spoke to them, as she had no intention of taking part in the ridiculous notion of colonizing anything. From the time of the asteroids discovery, their original plan was to have the entire family safely housed together in the Colorado military complex of NORAD. Patty was not happy that Ross had now wanted to splinter the family by altering that plan.

Several weeks before Ross' birthday, the aliens had provided Ross, and other world leaders, with the locations of where the transport ships would land. Two of the sites would be in the United States, so Ross had informed those people who were interested via a televised speech just exactly where those sites were. The aliens had allowed Ross to make the selection of one site, and he had chosen Washington D.C. The other site may have seemed strange to most people, but it made perfect sense to Ross when he also considered the ten other global locations.

To go along with the New Mexico desert near Roswell, the transport ships would also pick up passengers in Australia, China, Italy, and Russia. The locations within those four foreign countries, as with Roswell, were in areas where either a large quantity of UFO sightings had occurred throughout the years, or an alien scout ship had allegedly crashed. In most countries of the world that information had never been made available to the general public, but science teams and UFO believers began to put the pieces together soon after the aliens revealed the coordinates of their intended pickup spots.

Their other set of coordinates had revealed landing sites in remotely populated areas of the planet such as Nazca, Peru and Chichén Itzá, Mexico. Those locations were a mystery to Ross until he put them together with the two other more populated locations of Stonehenge, England and Ayutthaya, Thailand. The light bulb in his mind then shone brightly when he saw the final location was adjacent to the giant pyramids of Giza, Egypt. Those five locations each represented an area of the planet where long ago cultures had existed, and they each also contained elaborate ruins or monuments of ancient origin that had never been completely understood or explained.

Ross thought to himself that the Incan civilization of Peru could have been strongly influenced by long ago observational visits by aliens, and that same alien species was trying to help the Earth now. It actually made perfect sense, as the vast and strange markings on the ground near Nazca could only be recognized from high in the air. Their presence had always baffled historians, and they were only one of the mysteries of Peru. Add to that the substantial amount of ancient ruins at multiple sites that included Saqsaywamán near Cuzco, and the world renowned Machu Picchu high in the Andes, and Peru was loaded with unexplained structures.

The stones that make up the structures at those locations vary in size and shape, and some are larger than cars, but they are fitted together so perfectly that a piece of paper can't be pushed in between them. The current engineering capabilities of Earth can hardly duplicate that level of precision, and the Incan civilization didn't possess the computers to calculate, or the machinery to place such large and heavy objects into their seemingly perfect positions.

Similar structures of magnificent precision can also be found on the Yucatan Peninsula of eastern Mexico, and to the south throughout Belize, Guatemala, and Honduras. Those were built long ago by the Mayan culture, which suddenly vanished from existence seemingly overnight. Thailand, in Southeast Asia, also has huge temples and other structures from a more recent time in human history, but how they were engineered and built has yet to be fully understood. Ross began to see a pattern of perhaps several ancient civilizations having somehow been helped along by this, or another, alien species.

Although much smaller in stature, the Stonehenge site in southern England has also been a source of inquiry for many years. At that highly visited location west of London, huge stone tablets have been placed in a circular type pattern of some significance, but it is unclear as to their exact origin that dates back a few thousand years.

Finally there was Egypt, where the Sphinx and three giant pyramids were positioned in perfect alignment to either gaze upon, or symbolically represent a segment of the Orion constellation. Dozens of Earth centuries, and the atmospheric conditions of the region, had taken their toll on those magnificent ancient temples, but the craftsmanship equal to those of the previously mentioned ruins was still quite evident.

The only one of the eleven pickup locations designated by the aliens that Ross couldn't seem to get a grip on until recently was the one along the southern shore of the Baltic Sea in Germany. For some reason the small peninsula just west of the border with Poland had been chosen, but even the most dedicated of UFO followers couldn't provide the answer as to why. There didn't seem to be enough evidence of multiple sightings or a crash in the area to place Peenemünde within the group that included Roswell, and there were also no ruins to suggest an ancient culture as in some of the other locations.

During a teleconference meeting with government leaders from the countries with pickup locations, Ross learned that Peenemünde had been the location of Germany's rocket program in the late stages of World War II. It had been the birthplace of the rocket technology that had eventually taken mankind, including Ross, into space, but that birth had come out of a dark time in the modern evolution of mankind. Ross smiled while realizing the aliens had selected that location because it had been where an early major step had occurred in what made the inhabitants of Earth a so called emerging species that would someday soon be ready to explore the cosmos. Thankfully that same technology had not been utilized to completely destroy the planet since its development, although there had been a few times when it seemed imminent.

The current level of that same rocket technology had been put to the test of late, as NASA and other space agencies had been quite busy. Aside from the probes that had been studying the asteroid, many had been launched towards Mars. They were of course all unmanned, but they contained information about the human species and other life forms that inhabited Earth. The thought was that if all life on the planet were to perish, there would be a record of a civilization having in fact existed at some point. Some other species may someday discover the probes on Mars and learn about what had been, and what had transpired, here on Earth.

As for now, the leading military minds were preparing one last ditch effort to save the planet from impact by launching

236

nuclear missiles at the asteroid. The action was certainly worth a try, and it would make all the generals feel better to have flexed their collective muscles, but it would be a hopeless attempt. The data Ross had received from several leading astronomers of the planet had been quite clear that it was not enough firepower to significantly damage the incoming rock. Who would have believed that a civilization who at one point in time possessed enough nuclear firepower to vaporize the planet several times over, did not currently possess enough of that same firepower to save it by altering the asteroids course.

According to Ross' old alien friend, the transport ships would land at all of the twelve chosen locations with only three or four Earth days left before the asteroid impact, and would remain there for two days in order to pick up all those who wished to take part in the adventure of a new lifetime. The act itself would require a tremendous leap of faith because if the transport ships didn't show up as planned, most of the people waiting for them would be nowhere near an adequate shelter.

# 50

## *Departure*

One by one the huge alien transport ships began to liftoff from various areas of the Earth's surface with their precious cargo. As each one ascended with a group of humans who had made the choice to leave their home world behind, the lead ship of the armada made preparations to board the last few handfuls of the passengers assigned to her. The ship had landed two days before upon the vast section of lawn known as the National Mall between the Washington Monument and the United States Capitol Building, and the perimeter was closely guarded by a secret service detail and accompanying military contingent. In a few short hours former President Ross Martin, his sister Jessica, and his oldest daughter Aurora would board the ship with a small group of loyal followers that included a single secret service agent and Mrs. Patterson. They would then all depart for the great unknown of space.

Throughout the previous few months Ross and Jessica had pleaded with the rest of the family to join them on their pilgrimage in quest of the new world, but only Aurora had been swayed. Patty, along with the vast majority of the planets population, refused to believe in the good intentions of the visiting alien species, and had therefore opted to stay behind. The general belief was that the alien species simply wanted to take the human contingent back to their home world, and either perform hideous medical experiments upon them, or use them as forced slave labor. The thought process was in direct correlation to what people had viewed for many years on their television screens, computers, or in movie theatres, and Ross once again marveled at the power of the world media to shape public opinion.

Rachel had sided with her husband's viewpoint on the subject, and in spite of the extremely challenging future or possible death that lay in front of them, would stay on Earth along with their two children Luke and Janet. The family would be divided in a way that no one had ever imagined, but Ross knew he needed to be part of the surviving population that would help colonize a new world.

One thing that had surprised Ross was that there was never a need for some sort of worldwide lottery to decide who would be saved. From the very beginning of the process, the aliens had informed the people of the Earth that only a limited amount of room would be available on the armada of transport spaceships. For some reason beyond Ross' comprehension, so few people had shown any interest in colonizing a new world that a campaign needed to be developed in order to convince more people to take the journey. It had only been during these last few desperate days that many people had a change of heart, but it was too late for any of them to request passage.

At noon eastern standard time of August 22, 2022 Ross Martin resigned as President of the United States, and his former Vice President, Thomas Walton, assumed the role of Chief Executive. Ross had become only the second person in the history of the country to resign from the Presidency, but the circumstances were vastly different from what had caused the previous occasion. Ross knew that his former Vice President was a good man who would do his best to lead what remained, if anything at all, of the nation after the catastrophe. The former Governor of Wisconsin, had been on the ticket as Ross' running mate during both of the Presidential campaigns, and had been an instrumental part in assuring their first victory by helping Ross carry several key mid-western states with large numbers of Electoral College votes. Thomas Walton's many years of quality public service to his country had earned him the right to be the President even if only for a short time, so Ross was honored to hand him the reigns.

Some viewed Ross as a coward for leaving the office just days before the impact of the asteroid, but he didn't care. Within moments after resigning from office, Ross had retrieved the necklace from the reading lamp on his former desk, and had put it back around his neck. He then began a solitary walk within the walls of the White House that would take a few hours. He wanted to say goodbye to what remained of the staff and friends who had been so loyal to him throughout not only his years in the White House, but in some cases for decades. There were several people missing during his tour, as those who had accepted the New Year's Eve gift of a guaranteed spot in the Strickland's Colorado shelter had made their way west several weeks earlier.

The family was waiting for him upstairs in the residence so that everyone could say their goodbyes to each other in private, and Ross took that opportunity to present his now ten year-old grandson Luke with a very important gift. Luke had admired the fishing pole with the red bow on it every time he had seen it, so Ross thought it was only right to pass it on to him. He asked Luke to take care of the precious object as he reflected back to the day he received it from Grandpa Hank, and to pass it down to his own grandson someday if he could.

Aurora, who didn't want her not quite six year-old niece Janet to feel left out, presented her with a little white kitten that she had named Snowflake. The little girl instantly perked up at the sight of the kitten, and promised her Aunt Aurora that she would take good care of her new best friend.

Ross took the lead on what could only be described as an awkward situation by giving each of his grandchildren one last kiss on the forehead, and then his only son-in-law a firm handshake. Next was the goodbye hug with his youngest daughter Rachel, and she burst into tears when Ross asked her, "How many grains of sand are there on the beach?" Aurora joined in the hug with her father and younger sister, as she reminded them, "There were way too many to count!"

A moment later Ross, with tears welling up in his eyes, moved towards Patty to say goodbye to his soul mate of some sixty years. They had been through it all together and had held each other up through the difficult times, but they had also seen tremendous joy over the years. Ross had lost his grandfather Hank, father Robert, and best friend Dennis during his much younger years, while Patty had lost her mother Elizabeth and best friend Betty in more recent times. On the positive side they had raised two wonderful children, which eventually led to a couple of grandchildren, and had enjoyed the comforts of Ross' tremendous career path.

They held each other in a long embrace, and through the tears Patty uttered, "Please stay with me!" Ross returned the emotion with quivering voice by saying, "Will you please join me on this pilgrimage?" They both wanted to stay together so much, but they remained at an impasse as neither would yield. With a final passionate kiss, they said farewell.

Within an hour after the tearful goodbye, Ross and his group were preparing to board the alien spaceship. He waved goodbye to the well-wishers in the surrounding crowd, and turned to climb the long ramp leading into the vessel. As the last two people to board, Aurora carried the American flag from her grandfather Robert tucked under her arm, and Ross did the same with Grandpa Hank's. When the armada would arrive at their new home world, many flags of various countries would be flown to signify different cultures and nationalities associated with the human endeavor. Ross could think of no more fitting American flags to fly than the two that he and his oldest daughter carried.

Rising slowly at first above the National Mall, the alien transport ship began to pick up some speed to escape the confines of Earth's atmosphere. Many of the people aboard stood quietly at the large viewing windows to watch the planet grow smaller with distance, but almost all of them remained silent until the ship entered space. Several moments later the ship moved into formation with the rest of the armada at a safe high distance above the Earth, so the much smaller moon and quickly approaching asteroid could be viewed in their current positions on the far side of the planet. Jessica then turned to her brother Ross and told him she could finally understand the beauty of space, and why he had been so captured by the allure of it ever since they were kids.

People around them, from all walks of American society, began to gasp and murmur at the awe inspiring sight, and Ross felt confident that a similar reaction was taking place on each of the other eleven transport ships. Tragically, it had taken such an unfortunate event in the history of the planet, and mankind, to assist this new group of people in their understanding of what the astronauts of the past sixty plus years had all been so giddy about.

Ross had been informed by his old alien friend that the armada would remain at this location in high orbit until shortly after the impact of the asteroid, so that historical information could be obtained for their own data base. He also informed Ross that the message would be delivered to all those aboard the other ships in the event that anyone wanted to view the event.

According to the countdown the impact would take place the next day, but a startling revelation had just occurred to Ross. From their current position the Earth looked to be about the size of a basketball held at arm's length from ones face, and the Moon on the far side resembled a softball. Perhaps it was an optical illusion, or a final supreme act of denial, but the incoming angle of the asteroid looked as if it might actually miss the Earth by the narrowest of margins.

Ross wondered if it was possible that the tremendous gravitational force of our sun was having enough of an impact on the asteroid to drastically alter its course during these final days. Even if that were true, he decided it was probably in the best interest of all those around him to keep that thought private for the time being. After all, no good could come from creating some level of false hope among the other passengers.

# 51

## *Impact*

The following day Ross returned to the viewing window with Aurora and Jessica to find the asteroid much closer to the Earth, but the angle still looked a bit off. Knowing he probably only had a few hours until the impact; Ross informed one of the alien crew that he wanted to visit with his old friend before it happened. A few moments later, Ross was escorted to a more secluded area of the ship where he and the alien could communicate privately, and Ross asked him a series of very important questions.

Their discussion began with a reflection back to their first encounter on the Moon, as Ross said, "I never thought about why you were walking around on the surface." The alien had been searching for the emblem that he had lost when Ross had beat him to it, but the alien wasn't supposed to be out walking around on the surface in the first place. His old friend's thoughts informed Ross that he had wanted to get one more look at the planet before they departed for their observational rotation of this and the neighboring solar systems, but he had to do it secretly. That's when the alien lost the emblem, and he needed to find it again or he would have been in big trouble. What the alien didn't know until after Ross had responded to Dennis' shout of panic was that his commanding officer had come out onto the lunar surface looking for him.

Ross was now learning the true intent of why both of the aliens were out there, and the encounter with Ross and Dennis had obviously been quite accidental. Their species had wanted to minimize further contamination of ₹-829-૨ग-3, as there were already enough people on the planet who believed in alien life. That belief or knowledge, at least partly, had been because of the Roswell crash of 1947, but it went beyond that.

Ross remembered from a previous encounter, that the alien Dennis had encountered on the Moon was the flight leader of a formation that had lost one craft in 1897. The alien that Ross encountered had been in the same capacity when one was lost in 1947. What he didn't know until now was that one of the aliens that died in the crash of 1897 was the father of the alien that Ross knew so well, and had been the best friend of the alien that Dennis had encountered. That alien had then, out of guilt or loyalty towards his best friend, taken his son into his command structure. For the most part it had worked out, but there were occasions when it had not always been smooth sailing. Ross' alien had been forgiven for the loss of the scout ship in 1947 for obvious reasons, but had not been allowed back to the planet since that incident.

It occurred to Ross that the locations of the two crashes were very close to each other in terms of planetary geography, and he suddenly understood why. The alien that Ross knew wanted to view the site where his father had been killed in his crash, and the objective of the mission when he was the flight leader would take him close to that location. That may be why atmospheric conditions in the area of Roswell were ignored by the alien even after his formation was spotted in western Washington earlier in the flight, and that led to the crash.

Because of that completely understandable decision, he had been banned from future scouting missions of the planet surface. It turned out to be a costly decision for him, because if the alien wanted to have any future prolonged looks at the planet in solitude, his only opportunity would be to venture out on the forbidden lunar strolls whenever possible. It was probable that his commanding officer had known the alien most of his life, and had simply come out onto the surface to protect him from being found out by higher authorities. Everything was clear now, as Ross suddenly realized the emblem on his necklace needed to be returned to the son of the pilot who had died while wearing it. He took the necklace off, looked at his alien friend, and said, "I believe this emblem came from your father's uniform, and I want to give it back to you."

Feeling as if their relationship had been elevated to a new level, Ross said, "I have one more question for you." In responding to the all-important question of whether or not the asteroid would indeed impact the Earth, the aliens thoughts reminded Ross of his exact message when the two met in the woods of Camp David nearly eighteen months before. My superiors, some of who you have now met, sent me to inform you that, "The impact of the asteroid will alter the conditions that support life on the planet significantly", but you were never informed that the asteroid would directly impact Earth. The alien continued by adding that Ross would indeed be the last human to set foot on the surface of the Moon, because that is what the asteroid will crash into.

Ross staggered back a few steps and gasped in disbelief before regaining his wits, and then asked the alien to explain. He was informed that it was all part of the cosmic breathing process, and he needed to think on a huge scale if he was going to understand the truly big picture. The alien reminded Ross that planets make up a solar system around a host star, and millions of stars make up a galaxy like the one that both Earth and the aliens' home world are located in. Beyond that, a few thousand galaxies, with incredible amounts of space between them, comprise what is known about the universe. It is massive beyond the scope of most life forms imagination, including the alien species, and they had just begun to explore and map some of the stars in their own quadrant of the galaxy.

The alien continued by informing Ross that the entire thing expands and retracts like different life forms breathe, and during that process things are bound to crash into other things. In the case of Earth, an asteroid will crash into its only Moon, but this one just happens to be much larger than the thousands of others that have hit it before.

Ross understood the alien's meaning, because he had walked near several dozen of the many different sized craters caused by those uncountable impacts when he was on the Moon. The suspicions of many astronomers and scientists on Earth were then validated by the alien when he confirmed to Ross that ₹-829-4, or Mars, had been impacted long ago by an object large enough to render it currently lifeless. Ross then realized that the entire process of the universe could be summed up as one tremendously huge game of cosmic marbles.

Back to the impact of the present time, the alien informed Ross that they believed the force of the impact would break apart the Moon into several sections that would be unable to maintain orbit above the Earth. As Earth's own scientific teams have discovered, the asteroid measures one-tenth the size of the Moon with a composition that is quite dense with large quantities of iron. The force of the impact will be tremendous, and will push the softer Moon towards the planet as it begins to break apart. The larger pieces of both the asteroid and the Moon will crash down onto the planet over a period of several weeks in Earth time as the orbit decays, and each one of them will be catastrophic in nature. There will be huge surges in the oceans of the planet that could be thousands of feet high depending on where the impacts take place, and thick clouds of dust and debris from ground impacts will engulf the planet for several Earth years.

After all the larger pieces of the asteroid and moon have rained down, whatever is left of the planet will be in ruins. Food and clean water sources will be difficult to find after a short period of time, and Earth history dictates that some of the inhabitants will turn negatively upon each other. The satellite communications system in orbit will probably be severely damaged, or completely destroyed, from collisions with pieces of space rock that were either once part of the asteroid or the Moon. That will make it difficult for one region of the planet with survivors to communicate with other regions.

Much later, when everything finally settles down, the oceans will no longer have daily tidal surges because there will be no closely orbiting body to create the gravitational pull. That will have an impact on the ocean currents, which will in turn create tremendous deviations in the planetary weather patterns. The absence of the Moon will also eliminate a light source that has been used by the people of Earth when their position on the planet has rotated away from the host star. It may not sound like much, but with the thick engulfing dust cloud that will be created any light source at all would be a welcome one. At some point in the future the Earth may even develop a few rings much like the ones around ₹-829-6, because many of the smaller pieces of rubble from the initial impact on the Moon may remain in orbit. The rings won't be on such a grand scale, as the planet that you call Saturn is hundreds of times the diameter of your home world, but the concept is similar.

The alien concluded his current thoughts by informing Ross that in some regard the upcoming event will be far worse than if the asteroid were to make direct impact with the Earth. That would have been a tremendous punch to the planet that may have killed every living thing, but at least it would have been just the one impact. Ross remembered back to their communication at Camp David when he was informed that some people and animals would survive, but it would not be easy for anyone to do so.

Before Ross headed back to the viewing window where he had left Aurora and Jessica, he thanked the alien once again for all of his information and the help. If he wasn't already completely sure he had made the correct decision in evacuating Earth, the last twenty minutes would have convinced him. Ross' only regret now was that he had not been more persuasive with Patty and the family about coming with him, because this new information made their survival less likely.

Ross once again kept his new found knowledge to himself, and then watched in horror a short time later as the huge asteroid exploded into the surface of the Moon. After everyone took a step back in a purely reactionary impulse, several of them jumped for joy as they thought the crisis had somehow been averted. Some people claimed that they could return to Earth because everything was going to be all right, but Ross knew the horrible truth. He now needed to address the assembled crowd on hand, as well as the people on the other transport ships. He laid out all the information to those nearby that had recently been given to him by the alien, but before he could arrange a way to communicate with the other ships someone shouted out, "Look everybody", while pointing towards the window.

The distant moon appeared to be changing shape, and huge cracks in the surface were noticeable even from this distance as it was beginning to break apart into several large pieces. The end was now beginning, and it was going to take a strong stomach to continue watching. Within a few minutes most of the people, including Jessica and Aurora, had begun to move away from the observation windows towards their sleeping areas, but Ross stayed on.

The aliens were still collecting data about the impact, and then Ross felt a hand on his left shoulder. His old alien friend stood behind him while offering condolences for what had just happened, and then reminded Ross that all was not lost. Some of the people of Earth would indeed survive because he had been enough of a visionary to grasp the possibility of moving to another world. Ross had been the voice of reason by convincing enough people from various regions of the planet to join this quest, so somewhere between nine and ten thousand humans would now colonize the new world.

Another positive aspect of the adventure was that now away from Earth, the humans would age at the rate of the alien species while on the transport ships and the new world. That meant that for every twenty-five Earth years they would only age about a month, so they would all theoretically have many more years to live after the journey.

Before moving away again, the alien informed Ross that the data collection would continue for another Earth hour or so. If Ross so desired, the alien could inform all of the people on the transport ships that the armada would be ready to begin the long flight to the new world when that task was completed. Ross thanked the alien once again, and asked him to please relay the information to the other transports.

Soon after that Jessica returned to join her brother at the observation window for one last look at Earth, and they knew they were underway when they saw the Earth begin to shrink from view. They, along with a few other people at the windows, were amazed how fast their former home planet faded from view as the transport ships gained speed. As Ross and Jessica jointly contemplated the fate of Earth while gazing into the complete blackness of space, they noticed someone approaching them from behind in the reflection of the window. Ross' old alien friend had returned, and he was bringing them someone he thought they would want to talk to.

Although the alien would prove to be entirely correct, they did not recognize the person in the faint reflection. The woman wearing a green dress that perfectly complemented her long curly brown hair reached out her hand and with a velvety voice said, "Hello, my name is Janet Martin", to which Ross and Jessica exclaimed, "Mom?" as they spun around to greet her.